ARTHUR QUINN

QUINN

AND THE

WORLD SERPENT

ARTHUR QUINN

AND THE
WORLD SERPENT

BOOK 1
THE FATHER OF LIES CHRONICLES

ALAN EARLY

MERCIER PRESS
IRISH PUBLISHER – IRISH STORY

MERCIER PRESS
Cork
www.mercierpress.ie

© Alan Early, 2011

ISBN: 978 1 85635 827 9

10 9 8 7 6 5 4 3

A CIP record for this title is available from the British Library

Printed and bound in the EU.

CONTENTS

Dedicated to
Nana Moran,
who has kept every word
I've written

PROLOGUE

The agony is unbearable. Unbearable and endless.

His scream echoes through the cavern as another pearl of venom drops from the serpent's tooth.

The pan, once a source of brief relief, now overflows one drop at a time. The woman who emptied it is long dead.

He doesn't notice the limestone dust flutter down from the ceiling; he doesn't hear the rumblings of machinery above. And neither does the snake.

The single stalactite shudders. It draws the viper's attention. But too late. The stalactite snaps and falls like a rock spear, taking the snake with it and pinning it to the ground. It dies instantly.

He strains to gaze at the snake, his neck creaking. Despite the agony, and for the first time in more than a thousand years, he smiles.

CHAPTER ONE

'Ahh!'

Arthur Quinn woke with a start, disoriented. Sitting in the driver's seat next to him, his dad laid a hand on his shoulder and said something inaudible over the thump of music in his ears. He pulled his iPod earbuds out and said, 'What?'

'I asked are you all right?' repeated his dad.

'Yeah, yeah, I'm fine. Just a bad dream. A weird dream.'

'Yeah?' His dad fixed his attention back on the road. 'Weird how?'

'I dunno. Can't really remember it. Just this ... smile ... It doesn't matter.'

He popped his earbuds back in and stared out the window. A Coldplay song had come on; it kind of suited his mood. They were nearly there. Dublin. It had been an uncomfortable three-and-a-half-hour drive from Kerry, especially with most of their worldly belongings piled on the back seat and in the boot, and all that concerned Arthur now was a toilet break.

Arthur had shaggy brown hair and blue eyes flecked with green. Freckles danced across his nose and high cheekbones. He looked at his dad. With his grey temples and deep wrinkles, Joe Quinn appeared a lot older than forty-three. But then, he'd gone through a lot in the past couple of years. They both had. His dad's head started to turn and Arthur quickly averted his gaze.

Heuston Station passed by outside. People flowed constantly in and out of the building, hailing taxis and waiting for the next LUAS. Arthur reflected that, in all of his twelve years, this was the first time he'd arrived in Dublin by car. Every other time they'd taken the train, making Heuston Station their threshold to the capital. He could even pinpoint the last time he'd been to Dublin: two years ago, at Christmas had travelled up by train to go ice-skating: himself, his dad and … his mum. That had been just before she'd gotten ill.

He looked down at the ribbon tied around his right wrist and fingered it absent-mindedly. It was a pale golden colour, soft to the touch. The edges were neatly cut and hadn't frayed, even at the knot. It had been his mother's; now it was his.

As they drove along the quays it started to rain. Arthur looked past Joe at the drops hitting the River Liffey. The water was high and dark, reflecting the clouds above. Somewhere nearby was his dad's new office.

It had all happened so quickly – Arthur had barely had time to say goodbye to all his friends. Three days ago he'd come home from school to find Joe all flustered, making phone calls and filling out forms.

'What's up?' Arthur had asked as his dad finished the call he'd been on.

Joe looked at his son. 'Well, it's a long story.'

'What is it?'

'I got a call this morning. You know the new Metro line they're digging in Dublin?'

Arthur had of course heard about it. Who hadn't? The fact that Dublin was finally getting its own underground rail line had been front-page news for weeks. They'd been planning it for years and construction had finally started. Well, excavation had finally started.

'Yeah. What about it?'

'Well, they're having trouble excavating under the Liffey,' his dad had continued. 'Turns out the foundations aren't as stable as they first thought and they've had a couple of small cave-ins. Anyway, they've offered me a job.'

It made sense. Joe was an engineer with experience excavating tunnels. As a young man in the early nineties, he'd even worked on the Channel Tunnel, the train link under the sea between England and France.

'Cool!' Arthur had exclaimed. 'So what does that mean?'

'Well, for starters, it means we're going to have to move.'

'Move?'

'To Dublin.'

'What? When?'

'Well, Sunday. But –'

'What!'

'Look, Arthur, it'll be fine. They've found us a house and a school for you – it's a really good one. And it's a nice house, they've sent me pictures. I'll show you them later.'

'But –'

'Please, Arthur. It's good money. Really good. And it's only for six months or so. Just the rest of this school year, really. We'll be back here for next year, for secondary school. And I think a break from Kerry will do wonders for both of us.'

Without another word, Arthur had gone to his room and started to pack.

And now, driving alongside the Liffey, Arthur couldn't help but wish he was back in that room.

Willie Higgins inhaled greedily on his cigarette as the rain pattered on the roof of the security shed. The shed itself was very basic, consisting of four walls and a roof, all constructed from corrugated iron. A small Perspex window had been fitted in the creaky door, while the floor was a sheet of plywood that bounced slightly as he walked on it. The only pieces of furniture in the shed were the small yet comfortable wooden stool he sat on and the gas heater that kept him warm on days like these. He opened the *Sunday World* to the sports pages and started reading about today's games.

Willie was one of eight full-time security guards posted to the Usher's Quay Metro site. From here, the construction company, Citi-Trak, was excavating the first tunnel for the state-of-the-art Metro. They planned to have the tunnel complete within five years, an optimistic estimation in anyone's book. Ordinarily, work would continue fourteen hours a day, seven days a week, even on a Sunday. But work had been stopped on the previous Wednesday following a small cave-in in one of the secondary tunnels. Luckily no one had been injured – or worse, killed – but, nevertheless, work had been suspended.

Well, suspended for everyone but Willie and the seven other security guards. But Willie didn't mind. At sixty-two, he was glad to be out of the house, especially on a Sunday when all the grandkids were around, screaming their heads off. He had a flask of tea, his papers, some sandwiches and a radio. What more could he want?

'Excuse me.'

The voice startled him so much he dropped his paper onto the plywood floor. He had been so engrossed in the story he hadn't even heard the hut door open. He bent to pick the paper up, but the owner of the voice reached it first and handed it to him.

'Thanks,' said Willie and looked up at the speaker. She was tall – over six foot – with long blonde hair and wearing a slinky red dress. She had no coat on but held a black umbrella over her head. Against the grey rubble of the site through the window, she stood out like a sore thumb. No, that wasn't right – she'd stand out anywhere. She reminded Willie of the supermodels his wife watched on that television show. And now he saw the door was shut behind her but, again, he hadn't heard it closing.

'Jaysus, you scared the life out of me,' he said. 'Can I help you?'

'Willie, isn't it?' Her voice was smooth, breathy and had no distinct accent.

'That's right. Do I know you?'

'I don't think we've met.' She offered her hand. 'I'm Aidan Byrne's wife.'

'Oh, Mrs Byrne!' he exclaimed, shaking her hand a little too vigorously. 'Lovely to meet you! How's Mr Byrne today?'

'He's fine. Actually that's why I'm here. He forgot his jacket in the office – the feather-head.'

'Oh well then,' he started to pull on his rain jacket, 'let me get it for you.'

'No, it's all right, Willie. I'll get it. You stay here, nice and dry.'

He hesitated, one arm in the jacket. 'Are you sure, Mrs Byrne?'

'Of course I'm sure, Willie.' She held out her hand

and smiled. Willie unhooked his heavy bunch of keys from his belt-loop and placed them in her palm. 'No problem at all.'

❋❋❋❋❋

The Citi-Trak office was just over the crest of some rubble, barely out of sight of the security shed. The office consisted of two prefabs side by side. One prefab housed a kitchenette-cum-canteen and two small bathrooms, while the other housed the office itself. Without looking, the woman picked the correct key and let herself in.

Inside, papers and plans were piled high on desks. Blueprints were tacked to the walls, alongside computer-generated designs of the Metro trains and tracks. There were four desks in the room, each with its own laptop, and a large boardroom table in the centre. Along one wall was a row of tall filing cabinets. The woman slowly walked over to the cabinets, dragging her red fingernails along the nearest desk as she went. She read the labels on the fronts of the cabinets, eventually opening a drawer labelled 'Human Resources'. Her nails flicked through the files quickly then stopped suddenly. She pulled a folder out and shut the drawer with a clang that resounded around the prefab. With a laugh that would have chilled even Willie's warm heart to the core, she took the file with her and left.

***

While Mrs Byrne was gone, Willie returned to reading his paper. He received another shock when she peeked in at him through the Perspex window.

'All done!' she mouthed, dangling his keys by her face. Willie got up to open the door. The cold wind blew around his ankles and he pulled his heavy coat around him tighter, half-wondering how Mrs Byrne could wear something so light in this weather. She dropped the keys back into his open hand.

'Did you get sorted, Mrs Byrne?'

'I did indeed, Willie. Thanks so much.'

As she walked away over the rubble, Willie shuffled

back to his stool, trying to return his attention to the *Sunday World*. But there were two niggling thoughts in the back of his mind. The first was that Mrs Byrne didn't have a jacket with her as she left. The second was that he'd never heard of an Aidan Byrne.

As suddenly as the thoughts formed in his mind, they were gone. Just like the woman.

'Well, this is it,' said Joe as they pulled into the drive.

Arthur didn't want to admit it but it was true – the house was nice. It was red-brick, boxy but modern-looking. The most prominent feature was a large floor-to-ceiling window at the upstairs landing. There was no front lawn, just a stone-paved driveway. It was nice, all right. But it wasn't Kerry.

They got out of the car and, as Joe got to grips with the seemingly complicated unlocking procedure, Arthur took in his surroundings. The estate was reasonably new, with only a handful of other houses in it, all identical apart from the colours of their doors.

There was an open grassy area in the centre of the estate. He heard the thump of a plastic football being kicked and followed the sound. In the far corner, a boy of about seven or eight with curly brown hair was volleying the ball against a garage wall. As the ball bounced past him, he turned and noticed Arthur. The boy waved excitedly.

'Got it!' Arthur heard Joe exclaim behind him and he turned. Joe pushed the blue door open and Arthur followed him inside.

As expected, the interior of the house was as modern as the exterior. All open plan, white walls and cream carpets. The kitchen, on the other hand, was all stainless steel and flowing curves.

'It'll be like living in a spoon,' commented Arthur.

One good thing downstairs was the forty-six-inch LCD HD television hanging on the living-room wall. There were three bedrooms upstairs: the large master with a king-size bed and two big single rooms. Arthur and Joe took a single room each, leaving the master bedroom unoccupied.

For the rest of the day, they unpacked. With the

addition of his favourite posters, Arthur's new bare white bedroom now had a bit of life and colour in it, but it still didn't feel like home. Later they ate take-away pizza in a silence that was broken only when Joe eventually spoke. 'Looking forward to tomorrow?'

'Meh. You?'

'Yeah, Arthur, actually I am. This'll be good for us.'

'So you keep saying.'

Arthur went to bed early, even though Joe offered to rent a DVD for them. Apprehension over his first day at a new school kept him awake until after three, but he eventually fell into a fitful sleep.

CHAPTER TWO

In a time before written history, in Asgard, the realm of the gods, it is said that the great wolf Skoll chases the sun across the sky and that this is why the sun changes position throughout the day. If this is so then Skoll has just begun his chase, for it is dawn. The sun is still low on the horizon and the sky is a deep bronze colour.

Twelve gods and twelve goddesses reside in Asgard, ruled over by the one-eyed All Father, Odin. None of them stirs this early in the morning. They continue to sleep on their soft feather beds in their great halls. All of them are sleeping heavily after the enormous feast they enjoyed the night before. They ate wild boar and drank sweet mead till their bellies were full. All of them rest. Except one.

The Father of Lies leaves his hall and squints up at the brightening sun. The heat of it still hasn't reached the earth and a light dew has formed on the ground. He pulls his black cloak around him tighter against the cold, then makes off in the direction of the sea.

He has many names, the Father of Lies. The Sky Traveller is one; the God of Mischief is another; the Trickster God is another still. But his true godly name is Loki.

Asgard is a land of contradictions: beautiful yet barren, fertile yet rocky. As Loki makes his way across the rock-strewn fields southward, he recalls the feast of the night before. He spits on the ground, remembering the insult that the other gods inflicted on him.

A giantess from Jotunheim, the land of the giants, was the guest of honour. She was an ugly, dreadful beast, but powerful and strong, so the gods meant to befriend her. When Loki arrived at the feast, he was taken aback by the very sight of the giantess. She was obscenely fat, with lank red hair stuck to her brow with sweat. Warts covered her nose while blisters covered her hands and she had a shadow of thick bristles above her lip. Loki, being the God of Mischief, couldn't resist commenting on the vile woman.

As soon as he entered the banquet hall, he bounded onto the long feasting table and announced in his loudest voice, 'I knew we were having wild boar tonight, but I didn't expect one as wild or as boarish as that!' He pointed directly at the guest of honour, the giantess, to gasps and stifled laughter. Suddenly, the giantess leaped from her bench (the only bench large enough for her was a full-sized table) and strode down the hall towards Loki. She picked him up in her sweating, blistered hands and, before he could protest, she pulled a needle and thread from a pocket in her ragged skirt.

Loki wanted to scream but never had a chance. The pain was excruciating as the giantess went to work on him with the needle and thread. Most of the other gods looked on in awe, but All Father Odin didn't even look up from his meal. As far as he was concerned, Loki had insulted their guest and would get his just desserts.

When the giantess was done, she dropped Loki to the ground and went back to her bench, muttering apologies to the other gods as she passed. Loki struggled to his feet and pawed at the stitches that now bound his lips tightly shut. As he strained to tear the binding, a couple of the other gods started to laugh. Then more joined in, and more, until finally the entire banquet hall of the gods was full of laughter. Guffaws directed at him. Even the great Odin managed a chuckle.

Red in the face, Loki stormed out of the hall. On his return home, he managed to free his lips, but all he could hear was the echoing of the laughter in his ears. He vowed he would have his vengeance and spent the night forming the perfect plan. Now, early in the morning, he is putting that plan into action. He starts to smile at the thought of it, but his lips still sting from where he tore the thread out and the smile turns into a wince.

The sea rises into view before Loki, shimmering

and golden in the morning sun. The waves lap the shore lightly. A handful of small vessels are docked, tied to an out-shooting rock, but no fisherman or captain is in sight. Loki is glad of this as he walks over the sand towards the boats. He could have easily tricked any sailor present into giving him a boat, but he is anxious to set about the task at hand.

He picks the lightest-looking vessel to make it easier to row alone. With a quick slice of his knife, he cuts the rope securing the boat to the dock, climbs in and pushes himself away from land with the single oar.

Loki hums a tune to himself as he rows out onto the calm sea. He continues to row until Asgard is but a slim line on the horizon, then puts down his oar and stares into the clear blue waters.

His stomach rumbles at the sight of the cod and other sea fish swimming in circles beneath his boat. He hasn't eaten breakfast yet but that doesn't concern him now. He hasn't rowed all this way for mere cod.

All of a sudden, the schools of fish scatter. A predator has entered their waters. A sea serpent, about two feet long and with ribbed fins on both sides of its head, swims underneath the boat. Without a moment's hesitation, Loki takes hold of a net in the stern and drops one end into the sea. He watches as the net unfurls itself slowly in the water in front of the sea serpent. At first the serpent slows and turns away from the net. Then, for a reason unknown to itself, it looks up and sees Loki. The Father of Lies smiles at it from his boat. The serpent stops moving, hypnotised by the grin, and Loki pulls the net towards him, catching his prey.

Caught in the net, the sea serpent is instantly knocked out of its trance. It wiggles and shifts between the twines, making things awkward for Loki. He opens the net and drops the serpent on the bottom of the boat. It squirms towards the edge but Loki grabs it by the head, holding it down.

'Stop!' he commands.

The serpent at once relents. Loki grips it by the neck and holds it towards his face. As he stares into its slitted eyes, the fins by its head fan out threateningly. Its tongue licks the air and Loki mimics it with his own long tongue. The serpent's jaws shoot open, its fangs exposed.

Loki smiles then cautiously inches his index finger towards the deadly fangs. The jaws snap closed before he has a chance to retreat, piercing the tip of his finger. In intense pain, he drops the serpent to the bottom of the boat where it resumes squirming.

'That hurt more than I anticipated,' he murmurs as he takes a tight grip of the serpent again. He pins it by the neck to the base of the boat. The serpent screeches piercingly.

'You're lucky,' Loki tells it. He traces his bloody fingertip over the serpent's scales, drawing strange lines. They are the magical runes, letters and symbols designed to cause and trap magic. 'You will be my first. The first of three.'

When Loki is done, he lifts the serpent towards him again and looks directly into its eyes.

'I will call you the Jormungand.'

With that, he throws the serpent back into the sea. The water instantly starts to foam where the serpent entered it. Loki laughs hysterically and leaps up and down in his little boat, already rocking in the bubbling water.

The foaming grows more violent and spreads rapidly. Loki, thrown from his feet by the motion, holds on to the sides of the boat as it rocks over and back frantically, laughing all the time.

Just as the boat is about to tip over, the water abruptly calms. Loki stops laughing, out of breath. No birds caw overhead. The only sound is the soft lapping of the water against the side of his boat.

He looks into the water. It's darker now than it was, with a light coating of foam on the surface. Then he sees it: the serpent – his serpent, the Jormungand. And it is huge. Vengeance will be his, and that vengeance will destroy not just the gods but all the worlds.

Arthur woke up in a sweat, panting. He grabbed his mobile from the bedside cabinet and checked the time. It was 3.16 a.m. He sighed and collapsed back onto his mattress. So he'd only been asleep for sixteen minutes but had already had that crazy dream. That strange laughing man, the weird rocky land and now a giant snake thing!

He turned over and tried going back to sleep but soon realised that his sheets were damp. In fact, they weren't just damp: they were soaking. How did I sweat so much in a quarter of an hour, he wondered to himself as he got out of bed.

He left his room and followed the unfamiliar hallway downstairs to the living room. Arthur and Joe had piled cardboard boxes here which had yet to be packed away. He switched on the light and scanned the labels on the boxes.

'Office/computer stuff … Plans … Games and DVDs … Bed and soft stuff, etc.'

He opened the box of bedding to find it nearly empty, as Joe had only thought of bringing one set of sheets each. However, there were a couple of large beach towels tucked away in the bottom. Arthur thought they would do for the night – or what was left of it.

He made his way back upstairs. As soon as he

entered his room again, he was hit by something that he hadn't noticed when he'd left. His room smelled like the seaside – that strong briny smell of seaweed and salt water. As he moved closer to his bed, the smell grew stronger and more pungent.

Somehow his sheets were damp with sea water, not sweat. He pulled them off in a hurry, replaced them with the beach towels and climbed back into bed. As he turned over to sleep, he feared that his dream of the strange man in the boat had something to do with the damp sheets. And if that was the case, then what was that huge snake thing and why was he dreaming about it?

CHAPTER THREE

Brown. Arthur's new school uniform was brown. A brown itchy sweater, brown stiff slacks and brown uncomfortable leather shoes. Seeing no way around it, he put the uniform on and went downstairs to breakfast. Joe was already gone. He'd left a Post-it with instructions for how to get to the new school and a €20 note – 'buy yourself something nice'. Arthur wasn't hungry and left early, deciding it would be best to meet the principal before school started to keep the inevitable earth-shattering embarrassment to a minimum.

The October air was frosty and Arthur could see his breath condensing in front of his face. He yawned, still exhausted from his fitful sleep, although luckily he'd managed to catch a few hours after waking from that bizarre dream. He looked around at his new estate. Across the road a businessman with a laptop bag was getting into his Saab. At another house an old woman in a dressing gown was letting her dog out to go to the toilet. The dog ran around the lawn in quick circles, clearly not pleased about being watched by its owner. And at the house in the far corner the boy from yesterday was sitting on the wall, watching him and wearing an identical brown uniform. The boy jumped down and ran to his front door.

'Stace! Ash!' Even from across the street, Arthur could hear him calling into the house. The boy looked back at Arthur then ran inside, repeating the names.

Arthur shrugged his backpack over his shoulder and walked on. After only a few steps, he heard a door slam and turned to see the boy running down the street towards him, carrying a football and followed at a much more leisurely pace by two girls.

'Hi!' exclaimed the boy when he reached Arthur. He slowed and walked nonchalantly next to him.

'Hey,' said Arthur.

'Did you move in?' The boy was panting from his sprint as he spoke.

'For a little while, yeah.'

'I'm Max. Max Barry.'

'Arthur.'

'Hi, Arthur!' He pointed back with his thumb over his shoulder. 'They're my sisters. Do you like football?'

'You will soon,' said one of the sisters who'd just caught up. She looked about Arthur's age and wore her auburn hair in a neat ponytail. She was also wearing the ugly brown uniform. 'I'm Ashling. Ash.'

'This is Arthur,' Max spoke up for him. 'He just moved in.'

'Yeah, we gathered that, Max,' said the other sister. She was just like an older version of Ash – probably about seventeen – and was wearing a different uniform. 'I'm Stace, Arthur. Or Art, or Artie? What do you prefer?'

'Well, my mum always called me Arthur.'

'Arthur it is then.' She shook his hand.

Max was bored of all the introductions and, as they turned the corner onto the main road, raised the topic of football again.

'Yeah, it's all right. I kind of prefer basketball, though,' Arthur answered.

'Oh, well I love football!' Max went on. 'My favourite team is Arsenal and my favourite player is Fabregas. Do you know him? Fabregas? He's really good. Do you want to play football with me some time? Ash and Stace won't play with me and –'

'Soooo,' interrupted Ash as she clamped her gloved hand over her little brother's mile-a-minute mouth, 'you're going to Belmont?'

Arthur raised his eyebrows, slightly perplexed. She nodded to his uniform. 'Oh!' he exclaimed. 'Yeah, I am. Sorry, I'd forgotten that was the name of the school. Sixth class.'

'Me too! You're going to love Miss Keegan. Every Monday she does this thing where we study something in the news; it's so much fun. Stace goes to the secondary school –'

'In fact that's where I'm going now,' interrupted

Stace, turning off in the opposite direction with a wave. 'See you later.'

'And Max –' Ash continued.

'I go to Belmont too!' yelped Max, struggling out of his sister's grip. 'And I'm in first class and my teacher is Mrs McKenna and she's kind of old, like really old, but she's nice and sometimes she lets us play –'

'Football?' asked Arthur with a wry smile to a giggling Ash.

'Yes!'

Arthur took the ball from Max's arms and squeezed it as if to test its strength.

'Can you dribble the ball?' he asked Max.

Without a moment's hesitation, Max knocked the ball from Arthur's grip to the ground and tapped it from one foot to the other.

'That's all right, I guess,' Arthur said with the apparent knowledge of a talent scout, 'but most footballers manage to dribble the ball while running …'

'I can do that too!' Max dashed off ahead of them, controlling the ball as he went. A couple of pedestrians had to move against the wall or on to the road to avoid a head-on collision with the young footballer. 'Out of the way! Sorry! Thank you!'

Ash and Arthur burst out laughing. It took a few moments before Ash could catch her breath enough to speak. 'You've got a fan there.'

'Looks like it,' laughed Arthur.

'So where are you from? Why'd your family move?'

'I'm from Kerry. My dad got a job here. He's working on that new Metro tunnel. Not as interesting as it sounds.'

'And what about your mom?'

'She, uh … she …' Even after all this time, Arthur found it difficult to force the words through his lips. He looked at Ash and it suddenly occurred to him that she wasn't Paul or Dave or even Louise; she wasn't any of his friends from home. And that loneliness he had felt the previous night lying in bed came back to him. Ash was becoming blurred in his vision, as unwelcome tears filled his eyes. He looked away, ashamed of the poor first impression he was making, and looped a finger through the ribbon tied around his wrist.

Ash stepped forward and shyly patted his back. 'It's all right. Moving can be tough. So can … other stuff.'

He looked back at her, nodded and smiled weakly. They walked on to the bus stop, talking about nothing important at all.

Max was already sitting in the bus shelter when they got there, out of breath and clutching his football to his lap. 'I win,' he said through gasps, smiling as Ash tousled his hair.

A bus approached from the end of the road and stopped at the traffic lights. 'Just in time,' said Ash, counting her coins for the bus fare.

Then a strange thing happened that afterwards they couldn't explain. Déjà vu is an unusual feeling – like you're reliving a moment for the second time, as if the moment is a scene from a movie on repeat. But what happened to Arthur, Ash and Max was the opposite. Time didn't feel as if it skipped back, but rather that it skipped forward. When Ash looked up from her coins, she realised that the bus had somehow managed to pass them by and that they were the only ones left standing at the bus stop.

'Did that just –' She stopped mid-sentence when she saw who was crossing the road towards them. Arthur followed her gaze. The boy was also wearing the Belmont uniform. His hair was cropped close to his head, a pale, almost white blond, and his eyes were a sparkling, icy blue. He strode across as if all the world's share of confidence had been funnelled directly into him.

Arthur, who'd always been quite shy and modest himself, took an instant dislike to the boy crossing the street. He knew it was totally irrational to dislike someone before even meeting them – in fact, his mother had always warned him not to judge a book by its cover – but the cockiness the boy exuded simply striding towards them put him right off. No one should be that sure of themselves, Arthur thought.

'Will!' Ash gave the boy a brief but caring hug.

'Late again?' he asked when he stepped back. Max bounded up to him, starting to chatter away about football, but to no avail as Ash spoke over him.

'We missed the bus,' Ash explained. 'It was really weird.'

'I wouldn't worry about it. Who's this?'

'Oh, sorry! Will, this is Arthur. He just moved in across the road from us. Arthur Quinn, Will Doyle. He's in our class too.'

'Hey man, how's it going?' Will offered his hand. Arthur went to shake it in the usual way, but Will's hand moved in a rapid succession of hand motions and grips that Arthur had only seen in American music videos. He couldn't keep up. When the onslaught ended, Will sat down on the bus-stop bench. 'So, you're coming to Belmont?'

Arthur nodded silently.

'Cool, cool. It's not bad. Good gaff.'

'I'm sure it is.' Just then another bus pulled up. While boarding it, Will jostled past the others to get to the back row first. He lounged across two seats, keeping Ash and Max entertained for the whole journey. Arthur, meanwhile, pretended that he was very interested in the view outside the window.

Joe had spent all morning in the Citi-Trak prefab office poring over the plans for the Metro. He studied blueprints, maps – both geographical and geothermal – computer-generated images of the finished tunnel (complete with smiling passengers) and the white foam-board scale model that took up the length of three desks. Two junior engineers – Ruairí and Deirdre, both fresh out of college – were on hand to answer any of his questions about the site.

Ruairí was quite short and unshaven, with a ruddy complexion. It was clear from his overhanging pot-belly that he enjoyed a little more fast food than was healthy. Deirdre, meanwhile, was much taller, with a slender build and her hair tied in a bun. She wore thick, round glasses and it was clear to Joe from the moment he met them that Deirdre liked Ruairí quite a bit but Ruairí was too wrapped up in his work to notice.

Joe finished scrawling a quick note for himself then tapped a smooth mound on the model. The mound had little foam paving stones to indicate the pavement that would eventually be placed there, as long as things went according to plan.

'So this is where the latest cave-in was?' he asked as he tapped.

Ruairí nodded. 'That's where the latest – and worst – cave-in was. Though thankfully no one was hurt.'

'How can that be?'

'That no one was hurt?'

'No. The cave-in.' He pulled out the geothermal mapping for the mound area. The red and yellow swirls on the image showed layers of mud, bedrock and limestone below ground level. The mapping went three hundred feet underground, deeper than they were drilling for the tunnel. If something that would cause a cave-in had been there, it should have shown up on this image as a black space between the waves. Yet the image showed that the ground should have been solid rock all the way down. 'There's nothing here that indicates a cave-in was even possible, let alone probable.'

The engineers looked at each other in silence. Joe caught their look.

'What is it?'

'Well,' said Deirdre, 'there's more …'

In the open as they were, the wind howled against them, chilling them to their bones. Joe and his junior engineers were standing beside the mound in bright yellow hard hats. Tape cordoned off the mound, which was as even and smooth as it appeared in the model, as if no cave-in had happened underneath.

'How did you manage to fill it in so neatly and so quickly?' Joe asked, astonished.

'We didn't,' said Deirdre.

'Then how …?'

'This is how it was. This is how it always was. Even during the cave-in.'

'What do you mean "during the cave-in"?' asked Joe.

Ruairí and Deirdre looked at each other glumly.

Eventually Deirdre continued. 'I'm guessing no one explained the true nature of the cave-in?'

Joe shook his head, intrigued.

'Both of us were here that day – and about ten other engineers and excavators. We were starting a small dig on the mound, just some tests. Suddenly the ground started shaking. We could feel it underneath us, rocks falling away. We could even hear them crashing down below the surface.'

'We have some experienced excavators here,' Ruairí added. 'They all said the same thing: that it felt like a cave-in.'

'So we ran to safety,' said Deirdre. 'After a few minutes the shaking and crashing stopped. We waited a few more hours before venturing closer again. And this is what we found: the mound just as you see it now.'

'I don't understand. If there was a cave-in then all the rock from the surface should have fallen through. This mound shouldn't be level.'

'Exactly,' agreed Ruairí. 'But what's even more confusing is that when we did another geothermal it showed that it's completely solid the whole way down – as if there had been no cave-in.'

'Then it's faulty mapping.'

'It's not faulty. We've tested it elsewhere. And we've used different machines on the mound. All of them came up with the same result.'

'Solid. No sign of any cave-in,' Deirdre said. 'So what do we do now?'

'If it's solid,' said Joe, 'there's only one thing we can do. We start drilling again.'

Although he didn't want to admit it, Arthur was pleasantly surprised by Belmont School. The building itself was at least three times as large as his school back in Kerry and it was so new you could almost smell the paint. Ash explained that it had just opened that year; in previous years, during the construction work, they'd had to take classes in a variety of prefabs still situated behind the fancy new building.

As Ash had promised, Arthur found himself liking Miss Keegan. The young teacher seemed genuinely excited to have a new pupil – 'Another mind to mould,' as she'd joked – and she let him sit next to

Ash and Will in class. She wasn't even annoyed when they'd wandered in almost fifteen minutes late thanks to the weird time skip and Will's lazy stroll from the bus stop.

'You're late,' she'd said.

'No, we're not,' said Will.

She laughed to herself as if what he'd said made perfect sense. 'Of course you're not.'

Miss Keegan had strawberry blonde hair that fell in curls over her slender shoulders and she was wearing a floral dress that was probably too light for the icy October air outside. But she seemed not to mind as she strolled across the playground during break.

The day passed blissfully quickly. The most interesting part was when Miss Keegan taught them about what the upcoming elections would mean to the country. 'I like my pupils to keep up with current affairs,' she'd explained to Arthur. She called that part of the class her News-Watch. He had no problem catching up with the class and Miss Keegan even agreed not to give them any homework (a suggestion from Will on account of them having a new class member). Before he knew it, Arthur was walking home with Ash and Max. He waved goodbye to them as he went into his new house. He'd just shut the door when the bell rang, so he opened it again.

Max was waiting outside with his football offered up to Arthur. Ash stood at the end of the drive, smiling to herself.

'Fancy a game?' Max asked hopefully.

'Well …' Arthur said doubtfully. Max's face dropped in disappointment. 'As long as you promise to go easy on me,' Arthur finished, taking the ball from him and running to the open grassy area in front of the houses.

When Joe arrived home a few hours later, he was even more pleased than Max to see Arthur out playing. He pulled into the drive, left his work gear on the passenger seat and ran to join in.

That night, as Joe and Arthur slept peacefully in one house and the Barry family slept in another, mist swirled around the green. By morning the mist would have left a fine frost on the grass, but now only a tall, stooped figure stood there. Dressed all in black, the dark man watched Arthur's house, counting the minutes and biding his time. He could wait. He'd waited longer than a millennium already: what were a few more days?

CHAPTER FOUR

Arthur and Max's kick-around quickly became something of a tradition. Every day after school, Max ran straight to the green, dropping his backpack en route, and kicked the ball he carried everywhere to Arthur. At first Arthur begrudgingly joined in, but by Friday evening he found himself looking forward to the game. Ash was usually their sole spectator and sometime referee, but on Friday she was joined on the sidelines by Will.

Midway through the game, just as Max had scored his second goal, Will had come striding around the corner into the estate.

'Hey man!' he saluted Arthur as Max and Ash ran

to meet him. Arthur picked up the ball that Max had let roll away and joined them at the side. Over the past few days, Arthur had grown to like Max and Ash more and more. He found he had lots in common with Ash: they were both interested in art, they liked the same bands ('StinkPuppy is easily the best band in the world!' Ash had enthused, going over her iTunes library) and they shared the same sense of humour (neither were averse to gags about bodily functions and both adored a certain British sitcom where the lead character was a man in women's clothing). But while Arthur had hit it off with Ash, he just wanted to hit Will. Will was everything Arthur wasn't: boastful and confident to the verge of cockiness, he had no problem speaking out in a group or being the centre of attention. He even spoke in a slightly accented twang, as if he wanted to be a character on American TV, which he probably did. He usually addressed Arthur as 'man' or 'dude' and sometimes even used 'Artie', which drove Arthur crazy.

'Playing some footie there, Artie?'

'Arthur. And yes, I am.' He hoped Will would pick

up on the irritation in his voice but he doubted it. Arthur found that Will was always too wrapped up in his own life to really notice others.

'Will you play with us, Will?' asked Max, excited.

'I'm sure Will is far too busy to be –' Arthur started.

'It's not really my game, football,' Will interrupted, completely ignoring Arthur. 'I'm more of a basketball man, myself. Nothing like shooting some hoops.'

If this had been a cartoon instead of real life, a light bulb would have lit up over Arthur's head right then.

'Basketball?' Arthur said. 'Really? I play some basketball too.' He didn't add that he was more than a little good, having won All-Munster medals three times in his old school.

'Cool. We should shoot some –'

'How about tomorrow? It *is* the weekend.'

'That sounds good, man.'

Ash could sense the tension oozing from Arthur. 'We have an old basketball ring in the garage. You can use that. But for now, why don't you get back to the game? It's getting late and Max is getting tired.'

'I am not,' protested Max with a yawn.

Arthur was already running off with the ball. As he ran, Will shouted, 'See you tomorrow, man!'

'Looking forward to it. *Man!*' replied Arthur, relishing the thought of putting a dent in Will's cockiness.

The game ended with Max winning 5–1. Arthur had been distracted. He had only one thing on his mind – beating Will the following day.

The mid-morning October sun was uncommonly warm as Arthur crossed the estate to the Barrys' house on Saturday, dribbling his basketball as he went. Joe had had to go into work again, despite working all through the week. 'I still have a lot to catch up on,' he'd explained on his way out a couple of hours previously.

Ash opened the front door on Arthur's first knock. She pulled the door towards her by hooking the handle with her elbows. Her hands were covered in orange gunk.

'Pumpkin carving,' she clarified and led him inside.

Mrs Barry – whom Arthur hadn't met yet – was out shopping, while Mr Barry was taking it easy in front of the widescreen TV in the living room. He looked like an overweight, middle-aged version of Max and he grunted a 'hello' to Arthur as he passed.

In the kitchen, Stace was sitting at the breakfast table, glued to a laptop and updating her Facebook status. Bright orange pumpkin filling and seeds covered the other half of the table, where Max, in an apron, was kneeling on a chair carving a ghoulish face into his own pumpkin. He bit his bottom lip in deep concentration. Ash's pumpkin was looking good; Arthur recognised it straight away as being based on Edvard Munch's *The Scream* painting. They'd studied it in class in Kerry a few weeks ago.

'Stace thinks she's too cool now for pumpkin carving,' Ash said, 'so this one's yours.' She offered Arthur the last uncarved vegetable and a small carving knife. 'Go wild.'

Max helped Arthur hollow out the pumpkin with his bare hands – 'It's my favourite bit,' he'd said, orange slime dripping between his fingers. For the next couple of hours, they couldn't have been happier, carving monstrous faces into the pumpkins. Arthur was just appraising his work – an evil smiling face he half remembered from a dream – when the doorbell rang. Max ran to answer it and shouted back, 'Will's here!'

And so the game begins, thought Arthur, as he started to clean up.

***

They wheeled the basketball ring out of the garage in no time and stood it in the empty driveway. Arthur was impressed: though rusty, missing the net and clearly underused, it was regulation height with a spring-loaded ring and NBA players from a few years ago printed on the backboard.

Ash and Max sat on a low wall to watch and Arthur passed the ball to Will. 'You're up,' he said.

Will passed it back. 'I'll go easy on you.'

'No need,' Arthur said tersely. He passed it back with a little more force than necessary.

Both his mother and father had played basketball

in their younger years. In fact, they'd met outside the court after practice one night. Joe came out of the men's changing room, Arthur's mother left the ladies' and it was love at first sight. Arthur also had a special place in his heart for the game and had even managed to nab Most Valuable Player three years running in the Under-14 Munster League. He really didn't want Will to 'go easy on him'. He wanted to beat him, but he also wanted a challenge.

'All right. I won't go easy on you,' said Will. He launched the ball artfully over his head. It sailed smoothly through the ring. 'As the French say, *deux points*.'

The ball bounded into Arthur's hands. He turned straight around and flicked the ball back into the net. 'That'll be *deux points* for me, too.'

And that's how the game continued. Arthur and Will matched each other point for point, basket for basket the whole way through. If Arthur managed to score a three-pointer, Will followed shortly with his own. They'd decided on ten minutes a side and when half-time came the score was thirty-two apiece. They took a two-minute break, leaning against the wall with Ash and Max.

'Pumpkins, eh?' said Will, nodding to the three carved pumpkins Max had set up in the porch. 'I love the ghoul. And the smiling one is all right, I guess. *The Scream* is great. Edvard Munch, I take it?' Ash nodded, blushing. 'I love his work. It's just all so –'

'Right,' Arthur broke in, heading back out onto the temporary court, 'game on.'

The second half continued in much the same way. It was clear to both players and spectators that Arthur and Will were almost equally matched in basketball terms. With less than a minute left in the game, the pressure was on for either boy to come out victorious. Ego-driven, Will made his first mistake.

The ball was in Arthur's possession. He ran to the three-point position and turned to the basket. Before he could even set up the shot, Will blocked him, slapping the ball out of his grip and knocking into him with the force. Arthur fell to the ground, toppling backwards out onto the road. His phone dropped out of his pocket and smashed open.

'Foul!' he cried defiantly, leaping to his feet.

'Are you all right?' asked Ash in concern. She picked up the pieces of his dead phone. 'Your phone's seen better days.'

'I don't care. I'm fine. Foul.'

'Sorry, man. Didn't mean it,' said Will, retrieving the ball and handing it to Arthur. 'Take your free shot.'

Arthur accepted the ball and took his shot. The ball swooped right into the basket. He was now one point in the lead with twenty seconds left.

The game quickly resumed. Before Arthur was aware of what was happening, Will had taken possession of the ball. He ran at the ring, jumped straight up into the air underneath it and slam dunked the ball into the basket. He even managed to touch the edge of the spring-loaded ring with his fingertips as he fell back to earth.

Arthur stood aghast as Ash's mobile-phone stop-watch beeped, signalling the end of the game.

'Is that it?' asked Will. He'd landed on his backside after the momentous score and was getting to his feet.

'Who won? I wasn't keeping score.'

'You did,' said Arthur. He sat on the wall, suddenly interested in his shoelaces.

'I did?'

'Yeah, 56–55. You won.'

Will walked over and passed the ball to Max, who ran out and attempted his own slam dunk. Will put out his hand. 'Good game.'

Arthur, still looking down, said, 'Yeah. Good game.'

Will held his hand there for a moment longer. When Arthur didn't accept it, he shoved it in his pocket. 'Well, I'll be off. See you on Monday.'

'See you Monday, Will,' said Ash. When he'd gone, she turned to Arthur. 'Why didn't you shake his hand? That was so rude!'

Arthur looked up at her. He saw the disappointment in her face and then felt it inside himself. He was wrong and he knew it. But he couldn't bring himself to admit to it out loud.

'I don't know why people like him so much,' he said. 'I'm going home.'

As Arthur walked back to his house, he could barely

hear Max and the sound of the basketball thumping against the backboard over the guilty thoughts in his own head.

CHAPTER FIVE

As he got ready for school on Monday morning, Arthur was glad the weekend was over. Following the game on Saturday, he'd spent the evening in his room, staring at his laptop, waiting for his Kerry friends to come online. They didn't. He could imagine what they'd been doing: they'd probably gone into Killarney for a trip to the cinema or bowling. In fact, bowling was more likely this week. Sometimes they played in teams, but the teams would be uneven now with Arthur in Dublin, so they probably settled for solos. His screen remained blank all evening, Paul, Dave and Louise all marked as 'offline'.

After a week of eating take-away Indians, pizzas

and burgers, Joe and Arthur finally went grocery shopping on Sunday. Being Joe's only day off and with him not really 'in the mood for cooking', they ended up ordering a Chinese when they got home anyway. That evening, as Joe slept on the couch with a full stomach, Arthur had considered visiting Ash for company but still felt too ashamed to face her.

So, leaving the house on Monday morning, he was surprised to find Ash waiting by herself at the end of his drive.

'Hi,' she said.

'Hi.' He approached her slowly. 'I should apologise.'

'You don't need to apologise to me.'

'Then I should apologise to Will.'

'You should give him a chance. He can be a bit much at times but he's great once you get to know him.'

Arthur nodded. 'I'll make more of an effort.'

She opened her backpack, took out his mobile phone and handed it to him.

'You fixed it!' he exclaimed in delight, seeing its screen light up.

'Computers and electronics are my hobby. I've tweaked it as well so that you'll never run out of credit.'

'Wow! That's amazing. Thanks a million, Ash!'

Stace and Max were coming towards them from the direction of their house.

'Let's go,' said Ash. 'We don't want to be late another Monday.'

✶✶✶✶✶

The EarthKruncher 5000 drill had a seventy-foot-diameter conical point and could bore through half a mile of rock in just over a week. The concentric gorging swirls ended in a diamond-tipped point that was so sharp that no member of the drilling crew was permitted within ten feet of the drill without full body protection – hard hat, goggles and leather-lined gloves included – in case they tripped and fell near the non-revolving point.

The point was revolving now, though, at approximately three thousand rotations per minute, and the noise was deafening as it approached the rock wall before it. Luckily for Joe and the other crew members watching from a safe distance, they each had a pair of foam plugs squeezed into their ears which took the noise level down to just an irritating drone. They could still feel the soundwaves, though, reverberating through their bones.

As the drill started to dig into the rocky surface and a screech was added to the roar, somebody tapped Joe on the shoulder. It was Deirdre. She opened her mouth and shouted as loudly as her lungs would allow, but Joe still couldn't hear a thing. He shook his head, pointing to his ears, then nodded towards the exit. She led him out of the tunnel, past the smaller excavators and the crewmen setting up more work lights.

They came out into the sunlight, blinding after the darkness of the tunnel, and walked around to the top of the mound, away from the drill noise.

Joe pulled out his earplugs. 'What is it?'

'Luke Moran wants to see you.'

Luke Aloysius Moran was the millionaire CEO of Citi-Trak. From his appearances on several celebrity reality-TV shows and interviews in *VIP* magazine and on any chat show that would have him, the general population had a very clear idea of what he was like: brash, greedy, selfish and single-minded. It wasn't far from the truth. Since Moran's office had called Joe almost two weeks ago to offer him the job, he still hadn't had the pleasure of meeting the man himself, although he doubted it would be much of a pleasure.

'I'm busy. They're starting under the mound now.'

'I don't think he'll take "no" for an answer.' From the serious and slightly scared expression on Deirdre's face, Joe realised he'd better go and meet the formidable Mr Moran.

'Trains,' said Miss Keegan, spelling out the word on the blackboard. 'Tee-rain-ss.' She even drew a speeding locomotive underneath the word.

Will was already in class when they arrived. So unlike him to be early, but then he probably didn't want to have to face Arthur as much as Arthur didn't want to face him.

'Trains, Miss?' asked Ciara O'Connor, the class swot, in the front row.

'Trains,' Miss Keegan repeated, turning back to the class. 'News-Watch time. I thought we might look at the history of trains a bit this morning. Considering what's been in the news a lot lately. Anyone?'

A couple of hands shot up. Will answered without being prompted, 'The new Metro.' His eyes lit up when he said it.

'Thank you, Will. The new Metro.' She walked between their desks, handing out photocopies of a newspaper article all about the Metro. The photograph with the article showed the same computer-generated image of the finished Metro that hung in Joe's Citi-Trak office. 'And what can you tell me about it?'

'Well,' he said, 'it's a subway train, like in New York. It's going to run east to west under the city and, eh …' He couldn't think of anything else to say.

'Very good. Will's right. The first line is going to start in Dublin East, right at the coast. It goes under the city and comes out where?'

A few more hands shot up. She pointed to Ciara.

'Heuston Station, Miss?'

'That's right, Ciara. Now here's a tough one.' She went to the Dublin map the class had made a few weeks ago that was hanging on the wall. It showed all the main landmarks: the tall Dublin Spire, Heuston Station, the River Liffey and so on. She pointed to the coastline. 'So the tunnel starts here,' she pulled her finger along the map to Heuston Station right in the city centre, 'and ends here. But why have they started excavating here first?' Her finger landed right in the middle of the River Liffey.

Several confused faces stared back at the teacher. Arthur knew the answer – or at least thought he did – but he didn't feel comfortable enough to speak up in class just yet. Eventually Rob Tynan at the back of the class said, 'Is it because the tide is low at this time of the year?'

'No, Rob, that's not it. It's nothing to do with the tide. Interesting guess, though. Anyone else?'

As Brian Savage gave another wrong answer, Ash elbowed Arthur and whispered, 'Answer. You know it.'

'Ssh!' he said, elbowing her back.

'Something wrong there?' asked Miss Keegan. 'Ashling? Arthur? Everything all right?'

'Well …' started Arthur. 'Em … I think they're drilling there first because of the river.'

'That's what I said!' protested Rob.

'Not the Liffey,' continued Arthur, 'the underground river.'

Miss Keegan smiled and nodded. 'Go on.'

Arthur could feel his classmates' attention on him. 'There's this underground river called the Poddle. It actually goes under the streets and roads. Most people don't even know it's there but it is. Anyway, they have to tunnel below the Liffey and above the Poddle. And it makes it really dangerous, having two rivers there. If they started at either end the whole tunnel could collapse when they reach the rivers. But starting at the rivers, they can make sure that bit is safe before they do the rest.'

'Exactly right.' Miss Keegan's smile grew wider. 'You seem to know a lot about the operation. You must read the newspapers.'

'His dad is working on the tunnel, Miss,' said Ash.

'Really? Arthur, is that true?'

'Well, yeah. He's one of the head engineers.'

'He's kind of in charge of digging the whole tunnel!' exclaimed Ash. She looked at Arthur and blushed.

There was a burst of excited chatter in the class. It came to a sudden end when Will spoke up. 'Can you get us a tour?'

'What?' exclaimed Arthur.

'Well, if your dad really is that important, you could get us a tour. I mean, if he really *is* in charge, Artie.' There was a mischievous glint in his eyes as he grinned at Arthur.

'Oh, Will,' said Miss Keegan, 'that would be too much to ask. Wouldn't it, Arthur? Would it?' She looked genuinely hopeful.

Arthur glanced from her to the smug Will and without another moment's hesitation said, 'I'll ask.'

TUNNEL DRILLING UNSAFE

'I was nearly killed in the last cave-in,' says source.

Luke Moran dropped the newspaper on the board-room table. The headline seemed to scream out at them, next to a photo of workers at the Metro site with their faces pixelated.

'I'm not a happy man,' said Moran. He thumped his fist hard on the table. 'Not happy at all!' He was a tall, overweight man with large purple hands like undercooked steaks. His salt-and-pepper-coloured wig shifted slightly on his head with the force of the blow.

'Sir,' one of Moran's advisers sitting around the table spoke up meekly, 'I don't think we can do anything about –'

'I want this source *fired*!'

'We don't know who the source is,' Joe said reasonably. He, Deirdre, Ruairí and a couple of other engineers sat on one side of the table. Moran's advisers – all wearing identical grey suits and all excessively skinny – sat on the opposite side. Moran paced around the table at a furious rate.

'Well then find out! What are you, some kind of *idiot*? In fact, *who* are you?'

Joe stood up and looked Moran straight in the eye. He spoke calmly and evenly. 'Mr Moran, I am Joe Quinn. You hired me last week as one of your head engineers overseeing the Usher's Quay project. I and my son moved – at very short notice – to Dublin. You wanted the drill running again: today we started it up for the first time in almost two weeks. You called me here, away from the drill, as work was getting under way. Mr Moran, you hired me to do a job and I'm doing it.'

Moran stood speechless for a moment. No one had spoken to him like that in years, least of all an employee. He took a deep breath and sat down.

'You're right. Please, Mr Quinn, sit down.'

'You can call me Joe, sir.' He sat back down.

Luke Moran gathered his thoughts for a second, then continued, 'Joe, I'm sure you'll understand that this is a PR disaster. We're already overspending as it is. If word gets out that we're not being safe, we'll lose this contract. Can you even begin to imagine how many millions of euro we'll lose if that happens? Billions even!'

Just then, Joe's phone rang with his 'We Will Rock You' ringtone. He looked at the screen and wondered why Arthur was calling. It wasn't like Arthur to call during the day unless it was very important. He hoped nothing was wrong.

'I'm sorry, Mr Moran, but I have to –'

'Take the call,' said Moran with a dismissive wave of his huge right hand. 'I have bigger problems than you taking a call during a meeting.'

Joe stepped away from the table, pressed the answer key and put the phone to his ear.

'Arthur? Is something wrong?'

'Hi, Dad. No, nothing's wrong. It's just, this might sound weird but … well … Can you give my class a tour of the Metro site?'

'What? You called to ask me that?'

'Well I was in class and we –'

'No, it's far too dangerous. And please don't ring me for something like this during work again.' He hung up and sat back down.

'Something the matter, Joe?' asked Moran from across the table.

'No, it's nothing. It's just my son's class were hoping to get a tour of the site. Obviously it's too unsafe.'

When Joe looked back up, he saw that Moran was smiling broadly.

'No,' he said, 'it's not too unsafe at all. Call your son back, Joe. Tell him we'll give them their little tour.'

✳✳✳✳

Arthur was on the way back to class from morning break when his dad called him with the good news. He ran straight into his classroom and told Miss Keegan and then his classmates. They'd get to see the big drill, the plans, inside the tunnel and they'd even get their picture in the paper. The teacher was very excited and started making mental notes of everything that would have to be done in advance.

'We'll need to inform the principal,' she muttered to herself, 'and the parents, of course. And hire a bus. Oh, so much to do …'

Arthur looked at Will, expecting him to be sour-faced, but he seemed genuinely pleased about the tour. 'Thanks, man,' he said simply to Arthur.

CHAPTER SIX

'I want to see the drill. I saw pictures on the news and it looks huge!'

'I hope they bring us in the tunnel. We'll probably have to wear those hard helmets.'

'Oh, I hope we don't have to wear them. They'll ruin my hair.'

It was eight days later, a bright Tuesday morning and the class were in a cramped mini-bus, being driven away from the school and towards the Usher's Quay site.

Over the past week, Miss Keegan had been busy letting the principal know of their plans, printing off parental permission slips, getting them signed and returned to the principal's office and finally hiring the bus they were sitting in. The anticipation had been palpable. The class were the only children in the country being given this honour. But mostly they were looking forward to seeing the big drill. During the week, Arthur had tried his best with Will. He didn't want to be jealous of his confidence but that's exactly how he felt. So Arthur just remained civil with him. They didn't argue but they still weren't exactly friends either.

Miss Keegan was sitting in the front of the bus next to the driver. Since they'd boarded, everyone was having their say about what they were looking forward to most.

'Well, I just want to see the River Poddle,' said Will.

'The Poddle?' said Arthur mockingly.

'Why?' asked Ash, looking surprised.

'Think about it. It's an underground river. No one ever gets to visit it or even see it. I bet no one's been down there in a hundred years.'

'For good reason,' Arthur said. 'It's probably dangerous.'

'Danger's good. Danger's my middle name.'

'Either way,' Arthur said with a roll of his eyes, 'we'll never be able to get to it.'

'I bet we can find it,' Will said and turned away to look out the window. 'I bet I'll find it.'

When the mini-bus pulled onto the Metro site, getting past security with no problems, Arthur was pleased to see Joe waiting with a smile. A couple of younger engineers were waiting with him, holding a cardboard box each. The class bustled out and formed two lines as per Miss Keegan's instructions. She introduced herself to Joe, who in turn introduced them all to Ruairí and Deirdre. The engineers opened the boxes of hard hats and passed them around. Ciara O'Connor, who'd been concerned about her precious hair on the bus, was not impressed.

'Right,' announced Joe. 'Well, first of all, I'd like to welcome you all here to the Usher's Quay Metro site. I'm Joe Quinn – Arthur's dad. I won't be giving the tour but I'll be leaving you in the very capable hands of Ruairí and Deirdre here. Now, some rules for your own safety. Number one –'

Just then, a sparkling black BMW skidded to a stop next to the bus. The passenger door swung open and a tall grey-suited man stepped out. He opened the back door for the guest of honour, who was so fat that he struggled to get out. He stood up to his full height, straightened the wig on his head and beamed a bright smile at the classmates.

'Well, it looks as if we've been graced with the presence of Luke Moran, CEO of Citi-Trak,' said Joe.

'Nice to see you all,' Moran said in his booming voice. He rushed over to the teacher. 'You must be Miss, uh …'

'Keegan,' murmured one of his aides, sidling up next to him.

'Keegan,' he finished, 'Miss Keegan. So lovely to meet you.'

'Thank you,' she said, blushing.

'And look at all these excited faces!' He turned to the class, then clicked his thick fingers at the aide, who quickly proceeded to hand out gift bags with the Citi-Trak logo to each pupil. 'Thank you, Piers. Inside you'll find a cap, a T-shirt, a calculator, a pen and all the information you need about our great Metro project here.'

Some of the pupils pulled the T-shirts on over their hard hats: they read 'I love Citi-Trak' in bold black text. As the children sifted through their gift bags, Joe took his chance to speak quietly to Moran.

'I thought Ruairí and Deirdre could give the tour.'

'Not a chance,' Moran whispered back. 'I'm having my two best men give the tour. You and me.'

'But –' A couple more cars pulled up unexpectedly. A TV news crew piled out of one and a few photo-journalists stepped out of the other.

'This is the perfect photo op,' Moran continued. 'We need to show that the site is perfectly safe. So smile for the cameras, Joe.' He clapped his hands together. 'Now, this way please, children!' For such a fat man, his legs seemed lean and his long strides meant that the class and journalists had to half-run to catch up as he went towards the main site. The tour had begun.

As they followed, Joe took the chance to speak to Ruairí and Deirdre.

'I don't trust him for a second,' he whispered. 'Keep an eye on the kids at all times, in case any of them decides to go wandering off.'

Moran brought them straight to the office prefab. There was barely enough space for them all, photographers included, but they managed to squeeze in. They piled around the scale model of the finished project and studied it while camera flashes went off.

'Here we have what the Metro will look like in about five years' time when it's all finished,' Moran said, spreading his arms out over the model. 'You can see right under the ground there and through to the foundations – *safe foundations* – that we're excavating and –'

'Is that the River Poddle?' asked Will, pointing out a smaller tunnel running parallel over the Metro tunnel in the model.

Moran looked confused. 'You mean the Liffey?'

'No, he's right,' said Joe. 'It's the Poddle. It's an underground river. It wasn't always underground though. The Vikings used it a lot for trade and at some stage they diverted part of the river underground. We don't really know why. Maybe an early attempt at sewers – who knows? Either way, it runs under the city now. And you can see where it runs into the Liffey here.' He pointed out a small archway on the model. 'Usually the Poddle isn't much to look at; it just comes up to your ankles and is little more than a stream. But when the tide is in, you wouldn't want to be trapped down there.'

'Speaking of trapped,' said one of the journalists, looking up from his notes, 'can you show us where that cave-in happened a couple of weeks ago?'

'Ha!' Moran forced out a laugh. 'Cave-in? Is that what you hacks are calling it now? *Cave-in*? It was a minor incident in the excavation process. Just a hiccup really.'

'Can we see it?'

'Of course! Let's go and look at the site of the incident – *hiccup* – now.'

Moran had had the tape removed from around the mound, Joe discovered. Now it looked just like any other mound of earth on the site.

'See?' said Moran when they got there. 'Nothing at all unusual or unsafe about it.'

He stepped onto the mound and jumped up and down. For a man of his size, it was a comical sight and the class couldn't help but burst out laughing. The journalists snapped photos of him standing on the apparently safe mound, a self-satisfied grin on his face.

'Come on,' he said. 'Join me here. I'd like a photo with the children.'

The class clambered around him on the mound; Arthur, Ash and Will all had to kneel in the front. More photos were taken. Then they changed position, with Moran and the pupils all jumping on the mound at once – the perfect front page for tomorrow's paper. Even at this nothing stirred underneath them. The ground was clearly solid.

Moran bent and put his hands on his knees, out of breath. 'Now,' he panted, 'time for the cherry on top.

This way please.' He stood up and strode off towards the gaping tunnel.

※※※※※

The tunnel really was a sight to see. Though it wasn't that long yet, the earth walls had been reinforced with concrete and steel girders right up to where the drill lay idle. Everyone's shoes squeaked on the temporary asphalt surface beneath them. A few crewmen were securing a girder by the entrance and bright orange sparks flew through the air.

'Here we are,' Moran said, his voice echoing off the high ceiling, 'in the belly of the beast, as it were.'

'So we're underneath the Liffey now?' enquired Miss Keegan.

'No, we haven't drilled that deep yet,' answered Joe. 'It's a long process. Right now, we're just over the Poddle. In fact, if you put your ear to that grate over there you should be able to hear the running water.'

The class piled around an iron grate in the floor by the wall. It was circular, about two feet in diameter. A ladder went down from the grate into pure darkness. Arthur held his breath, as did his classmates, to hear the faint trickling of the River Poddle. He could just about hear dripping, distant and echoing.

'Now, I think we should take a look at the big drill!' exclaimed Moran, marching towards the massive machinery. Miss Keegan and Joe promptly went with him, followed by the class members, engineers, advisers and journalists. Everyone followed him but Will. When Arthur turned back, he saw him still kneeling by the grate, his ear pressed to the iron grille.

'Look at him!' Arthur said to Ash. They stopped and waved at him to come. Deirdre noticed them and joined in.

'Come along there!' she called. Will got up and begrudgingly went after her. As they walked on to catch up with the others, Will couldn't help but notice how Deirdre kept looking at the other engineer, Ruairí. There was a definite look of longing in her eyes. Will smiled to himself, seeing his chance.

'I think he likes you,' Will said.

'What?' said Deirdre. 'I don't know what you mean!'

'I think that Ruairí guy likes you. You should ask him out.'

'No, he doesn't. Does he? Should I?' She suddenly became flustered. Arthur and Ash looked at each other, confused.

'You definitely should,' Will said. 'You should ask him now.'

'Actually, I think I will!' Deirdre giggled and sped off to speak to Ruairí. Will immediately turned and ran back to the grate.

'Will!' Arthur whispered. Will ignored him, falling to his knees by the grate once more.

'Come back!' Ash called. He looked up at them and, without another word, pried the grate cover from the ground. He winked, then climbed down the ladder into the blackness.

'Come back, Will!' Ash hissed again. She and Arthur ran to the hole and looked down. They could just make out the top of Will's head as he descended the rungs of the ladder. His head seemed to fade, taken by the darkness. 'Will!'

Abruptly, Will's voice called from down below,

'Come down! It's the river!'

'Will, get up here!' Arthur tried now.

'No, you come down here.' They heard him splashing around in some water and laughing.

Arthur turned to Ash. 'I'm going to get Miss Keegan.'

As he turned to head after the teacher, the splashing below suddenly stopped.

'Why don't you come down here, Artie?' Will called out. 'Don't tell me you're chicken?'

Arthur stopped in his tracks, seeing red. Will had gone too far now. It was time to prove to the cocky little twerp that he was as adventurous as anyone. Without another word, he turned back, took hold of the first rung and started lowering himself into the hole.

'Now where are *you* going?' Ash exclaimed, grabbing his jumper and pulling him off the ladder.

'I'm going to make sure the idiot doesn't hurt himself. You go and get Miss Keegan.'

'Eh, no! If you go, I'm going. End of. Just because I'm a girl you think I should stay up here?'

'No, that's not it at all, it's just –'

'Come on down, Ash!' Will called up.

'Okay,' Arthur said, 'let's go.'

However, as they started the climb downwards into the dark, he suddenly got the distinct feeling that this wasn't such a good idea after all, but it was too late to turn back. If he did he would never hear the end of it from Will, and what would Ash think of him?

'Hey,' exclaimed Deirdre as she caught up with Ruairí, 'enjoying the tour?'

'Yeah, it's all right,' he said, kicking a stray lump of rock down the tunnel towards the rest of the group. 'We could be spending our time better though. I keep thinking of all the plans I have to file today.'

'I guess.' Her mouth suddenly felt very dry as she looked at him. She loved his cute, fat little cheeks hidden behind that manly yet uneven facial hair. She took a deep breath, 'I just wanted to ask if you'd like to come with me for coffee some time maybe into town and then maybe a movie or whatever you'd like even a walk along the beach no pressure just if you wanted to it might be fun what do you say?' She said it all in one quick breath and was now panting.

Ruairí took a considered moment to answer. 'Eh,' he said, 'well, it's not really a good time, is it? I mean, we're so busy with work at the minute.'

'Yeah,' she agreed, dejected, 'yeah, actually, you're right. Work. Important. Never mind.'

'All the plans I have to file today. And this tour going on. We're so busy these days. Another time.'

'Sure. Another time.' Deirdre plunged her hands into her pockets, hoping her disappointment didn't show on her face. By now she'd totally forgotten about the three stragglers.

※※※※

Arthur could feel rust on the cold iron of the ladder. There was also a very unpleasant smell of sewage which grew stronger as he descended. His eyes slowly adjusted to the gloom but he still couldn't see further than a couple of feet in front of his face. Ash stepped off the ladder and straight into a puddle.

'Ew!' she said, as she jumped out of it and onto a dry patch next to Will. Arthur climbed gingerly from the ladder and stood beside them. He looked back up and could see the small spot of light from the tunnel above. From here it looked like they'd climbed about forty feet down. Ash took out her mobile phone and put on the flashlight function. The two boys followed her lead and lit up theirs.

The electronic blue lights allowed them to see more. They were in a smaller, arched tunnel. The ceiling was low enough for Arthur to reach up and touch. Old, stained bricks formed the walls on either side and slimy, stringy gunk hung off them. The river itself was, as Joe had said, little more than a stream now. The water was only a couple of inches deep and a couple of feet wide. They were standing on a brick ledge barely above water level.

'The Poddle is just a puddle,' joked Will. Ash and Arthur looked back at him speechless. 'What? It's funny. Let's go explore.'

'No,' said Arthur, 'we're going back.'

'Are you afraid, Artie?' Will turned and walked off, following the flow of the river. Arthur clenched his fists and walked behind him, along with Ash.

The deeper they went, the more worried Arthur felt. In some parts the water over the years had worn the ledge to a smooth, slippery curve. In other parts even smaller streams gurgled from under the ledge, joining the river. The stench grew worse over these inlets – a mixture of over-boiled cabbage, raw sewage and rotten eggs. What worried Arthur most, though, was that they hadn't passed another ladder. In other words, there was no exit except the ladder they had come down and they were moving further and further away from it.

Eventually, Will stopped walking.

'Hmm,' he said, looking ahead.

'What is it? Oh …' Arthur said as he strained to look past Will. The river split down two tunnels, one running to the left, the other to the right. Both led to further darkness.

'Which way?' Ash asked when she saw the two tunnels.

'I don't know,' said Will. 'I guess we just pick one.' He wiggled his index finger between the two options. 'Eeny, meeny, miny and that makes this one mo.' He continued walking down the tunnel on the right. The others followed once more.

Further along this second tunnel, the water started to lap over the top of the ledge, soaking their shoes. Arthur really hoped that reason for this was that the ledge was lower here and not that the water was rising. A minute later, Ash spoke up. 'Will, I think we should go back. This is dangerous.'

'Are you joking, Ash? This has just gotten interesting. Haven't you noticed the walls?'

Arthur had noticed the walls but didn't want to bring them up. In the first tunnel, the walls had been clearly built from bricks. But in this tunnel, there were no bricks. This tunnel was carved straight out of rock. Clinging to the wall as he walked along, Arthur had even felt some rough patches where the carving wasn't as smooth. And now he noticed a few weird patterns carved into the rock – swirls and circles and strange letters that were part of no alphabet Arthur understood. But he did recognise them. He vaguely remembered them from the dream he'd had with the snake over a week ago. And that terrified him.

'Okay, I agree with Ash,' said Arthur. 'I really think we need to go back now.'

'Come on, guys,' protested Will, 'we don't know what we'll find if we keep going.'

'Please, Will,' Ash pleaded, 'let's go back. The water's over my ankles now.'

'It won't flood that quickly.'

Arthur had a sudden image of the place flooding very rapidly, of water rushing down the tunnels, of being trapped in this stone prison.

'*Will!*' he said with as much urgency as he could muster. 'We're not going any further. End of.' His voice echoed through the tunnel: '–ill, –ill, –ill, –ill,' it said.

'I'm sorry,' said Will, 'you're right. We should go back.'

'Thank you,' Arthur said, turning to go the way they'd just come. Then from across the river a glint caught his eye. He looked over and saw that the light from his phone was reflecting off something embedded halfway up the wall. He was already up to his ankles in murky water so he just stepped off the ledge into the river, soaking himself up to his shins.

'Arthur, what are you –' started Will.

'Sshh,' said Arthur as he waded across the river. The water was cool around his legs but he barely noticed it. All his attention was fixed on the thing stuck in the wall. It was circular, about twice the size of a two euro coin and made of bronze. There was a little loop at the top of the circle, which reminded Arthur of a pendant on a necklace. An image was embossed into the circle. It depicted a gnarled tree, three thick roots extending over the edge of the pendant and its branches intertwined over the top. There was something wrapped around the tree. At first Arthur thought it was a rope, but when he held the light closer he saw it was a snake. He reached out and touched the pendant. It fell straight into the palm of his hand, as if the old stone was barely holding it in place.

Will and Ash stood behind him in the river, looking at the pendant he held.

'What is it?' asked Ash.

'Look,' Will said.

'I see it.'

'No! *Look!*' He pointed down the tunnel at the way they'd come. A wave of water was rushing at high speed towards them. They didn't even have time to react before the wave crashed into them, knocking them onto their backsides in the river.

Arthur managed to get to his feet and helped Ash to hers. The water level was now just below their chests and rising rapidly.

'Where's Will?' she said.

Arthur looked around frantically and spotted a dark figure bobbing under the water. He quickly pulled Will out. There was a trickle of blood running down his forehead where he'd knocked it on the stone floor.

'Will, are you all right?'

Will shook his head to clear it. 'Yeah, yeah. I was just a bit dazed. Thanks.'

'Can you walk?' Will nodded his head. 'Good, we need to get out of here quick. The water is going to be over our heads soon.'

As quickly as they could, they waded back up the tunnel. With the water so high and the flow so strong, it was hard work. They all slipped more than once and, to counteract this, put their arms around each other as they walked. By the time they reached the place where the tunnel split, the water had risen to their necks. They didn't even see or hear the second wave coming until it was too late. This one was coming up the tunnel from the direction of the Liffey and it smashed into them, tumbling them head over heels.

Swept off their feet by the furious wave, they were instantly disorientated. Their phones, which had managed to survive the first onslaught, blinked out the instant the second wave hit. They didn't know what was up and what was down and soon lost their grip on each other. The only thing that Arthur was aware of was that he was still holding the bronze pendant. For some reason he thought that was very important.

When the wave subsided a bit, Arthur swam to a wall and clawed his way along the bricks, finding his way to the ceiling. The tunnel was nearly totally flooded but there was still a small pocket of air up there and he inhaled greedily. Will had also managed to find the air pocket.

'Have you seen Ash?' he asked Arthur.

Arthur just shook his head, preserving his oxygen. He took a deep breath and plunged his head back under the water. He could just make out Ash struggling on the bottom of the tunnel, pulling at her leg urgently. Arthur resurfaced.

'I think her leg's caught on something,' he said. 'She needs our help.' Taking another deep breath, he and Will dived back under and swam to Ash. Her eyes seemed to be bulging as she pointed furiously to her foot. It was caught inside a gutter on the floor of the tunnel.

Arthur swam closer to investigate more. If she pushed in her leg and turned her foot at an angle, it would come free. He took hold of her shin and tried to push it into the gutter more; it was the only way she could get the space to angle her foot. She shook her head in fear and tried pulling away from him. Will saw what Arthur was attempting to do and tried to calm her down, pointing to the gutter and giving her a thumbs up. Ash closed her eyes, refusing to look. Arthur eased her foot further into the gutter, turned it forty-five degrees towards her, then pulled it out in one smooth motion. Arthur and Will swam her up to the surface.

She pulled air into her lungs and gasped appreciatively. 'Thank you, thank you so much.'

'We're not out yet,' said Arthur.

'I'm so sorry,' Will said. 'I got us into this.' He looked to be on the verge of tears.

'It's all right, we'll get out,' Arthur said, trying to comfort them, although not feeling so sure himself.

'What are we going to do?' cried Ash. 'We'll never be able to hold our breath long enough to swim back to the ladder and this air pocket isn't going to last forever!'

Arthur could see the panic welling in both his friends and racked his brains to come up with a plan. Suddenly he had it. 'Do you remember what my dad said in the office about the Poddle?' Will and Ash shook their heads dumbly. 'It runs into the Liffey – that's where these waves are coming from, and from the force of them the entrance must be fairly nearby. We can get out that way instead.' The air pocket was now rapidly disappearing and they had to lean their heads back just to catch a breath.

'It's better than waiting here to drown,' gasped Ash. 'Let's try it.'

'Great. But right now we should take a deep breath.'

'Why?' They turned around to see a third wave rushing towards them. They just had time to grab hold of each other with one hand and brace themselves against the wall with the other when the wave smashed into them knocking them all back under the water.

Toppling head over heels through the water, Arthur was sure that these would be his last few minutes alive. He thought of Joe, wandering around back on the surface, probably looking for him and wondering where he'd gotten to. He thought of Miss Keegan, the young teacher who was sure to get into huge trouble now that three of her pupils had gone missing. He thought of his mother. Then in the darkness, he saw a rapidly approaching pinpoint of light. For a moment

Arthur thought, this is it. I'm dying and that's Heaven. But it wasn't Heaven. It was even better!

It was an archway. And through the archway was the outside world and the River Liffey. This was the point where the Poddle joined the Liffey. For a moment his heart soared and then they crashed into the iron grate that covered the archway, something Arthur hadn't anticipated. Still underwater, the three of them looked up through the Liffey and saw the bright blue sky, sunlight filtered but glorious, yet horribly unattainable.

As more water rushed from behind them, Arthur pushed desperately at the grate. It didn't budge. He pulled at it: still no movement. He started shaking it, panicking. It would be terrible to come so close to survival and for it all to end here. Ash saw what he was trying to do and wrapped her hands around the grate just below Arthur's, pulling at it with him. It remained firmly stuck in place. Then Will joined in the fight. They all closed their eyes, grunting, putting all their strength behind them, praying that the grate would open. Suddenly there was a blinding flash of green light. It was so bright they could still see it behind their eyelids when they closed their eyes. And with that flash, the grate fell apart in their hands. It crumbled as if it was nothing more than a biscuit that had been over-dipped in tea and fell to the riverbed.

For a brief moment, Arthur, Ash and Will forgot that they were in mortal danger and just looked at the pieces of the grate floating down into the depths of the Liffey. Then the sunlight caught Arthur's eye. He gestured upwards and they swam to the surface, inhaled deeply and found that they had emerged in the heart of Dublin.

CHAPTER SEVEN

'You are in so much trouble, Mister!' Joe said when he came into the hospital ward. He fell to his knees and wrapped his arms adoringly around Arthur. 'So much trouble.'

When they'd surfaced in the River Liffey, some Japanese tourists taking photos from the Ha'penny Bridge had spotted them. They ran around to the boardwalk and threw a lifebuoy in. Arthur, Will and Ash each clung onto the floating ring with one arm as the tourists pulled them in. They climbed an iron ladder to dry land and safety.

'Lucky I took swimming lessons last summer,' Ash remarked as they climbed, 'although Max refused to learn.'

A passing garda saw the kerfuffle and instantly called for a squad car. They piled in through the back door of the car, soaking the seat in the process. With sirens ringing and blue lights flashing, the car sped off to the nearby St James's Hospital. En route, the garda sitting in the passenger seat had questioned them, asking how they'd ended up in the river and what adults had been taking care of them. Between them they'd explained as well as they could: being curious about the underground river, the tide coming in, escaping to the Liffey. Naturally, they'd left out the part about the mysterious pendant. Satisfied with their answers, the garda had radioed the station, asking that Joe Quinn at Citi-Trak and Miss Keegan be informed of the children's whereabouts.

When they'd reached St James's Accident and Emergency Department, a nurse hurriedly ushered them into hot showers and left out warm hospital pyjamas for them. They were sitting in a small and empty canteen the nurses used, sipping hot chocolate, wearing the pyjamas with towels wrapped around their shoulders when Joe, Miss Keegan and the two engineers, Ruairí and Deirdre, all rushed in.

'So, so, so much trouble,' Joe said again as he kissed Arthur on the forehead.

'What were you all thinking?' demanded Miss Keegan standing behind Joe.

'We ... we weren't,' Ash said.

'Whose idea was it?'

Arthur and Ash's eyes met in silence. Will was about to speak up when Arthur interrupted him. 'All of ours,' he said. Will looked in surprise at the other two. There was now a plaster over his left eyebrow where he'd knocked his head in the tunnel.

'I'm so sorry, Joe,' said Deirdre.

'We both are,' added Ruairí. 'We don't know how they got away from us.'

'You were just distracted,' Ash said, then quickly added, 'by some other kids. It wasn't their fault, Mr Quinn.'

'Well, you're all okay now. Apart from the odd cut or bruise. But either way, it was a really stupid and dangerous thing to do,' said Joe, getting to his feet and totally missing the secret glances between the three children. He turned to the engineers. 'You two can go back to the site. Thanks for coming with us but it looks like we've got everything under control here.'

They told Joe to give them a call if he needed anything, nodded quick goodbyes to the kids and left. On their way out, they met a garda coming into the canteen.

'Excuse me,' he said, standing in the doorway, 'Mr Quinn? Miss Keegan? Can I speak to you for a minute?'

'We'll be right back,' said Miss Keegan, pointing her finger at all three of them. 'Don't go looking for any underground rivers while we're away.' They stepped out of the room, shutting the door behind them.

'Thank you,' said Will. 'You didn't have to do that.'

'It's as much our fault for following you,' Arthur said.

They sat in silence for a moment before Ash said, 'Your dad didn't seem too angry. Mine will kill me when he finds out I lost my new phone. Plus all the life-endangering stuff.'

'He's just relieved now,' said Arthur, 'but when we get home he'll probably ground me for life.' He turned to Will. 'What about your dad?'

'My dad's dead.'

'Oh, I …'

'It's okay. He died a few years ago. In a car crash.'

'I'm so sorry, Will. I … I know how it feels.'

'You do?' asked Ash.

'Yeah, I do. My … my mum passed away in … in March.' Out of habit, he fingered the ribbon tied around his wrist.

'Oh, Arthur!' She laid her hand over his. 'I kind of guessed but didn't want to ask.'

'It's tough,' said Will. He looked at Arthur directly, tears glistening in his eyes. 'And it doesn't get much easier with time.'

Arthur nodded.

'I'm sorry,' Will said.

'It's okay.'

'No. I'm sorry for how I acted.' He put his hand out to Arthur. 'Fresh start, Artie?'

'It's Arthur.'

'Fresh start, Arthur?'

Arthur took Will's hand and shook it firmly, optimistically. 'Fresh start, Will.'

Just then he remembered the pendant. He picked up his soaking trousers from where they'd been lying by his feet and pulled the pendant out of the pocket. It hadn't been damaged by the flood, but then it had probably spent years under the water anyway, maybe hundreds of years. Even though it was no larger than the palm of his hand, it felt heavy – or rather, heavier than it should have been. Denser, somehow. Will and Ash shuffled their seats in for a closer look.

'Can I see it?' Ash put out her hand and Arthur gave it to her. She held it up and scrutinised it.

'It looks like bronze,' said Will. Ash offered it to him but he declined. She looked at it again.

'Well, it's definitely some kind of pendant for a necklace,' she said, handing it back to Arthur, 'but what's with the rope and the tree?'

'It's not a rope,' Arthur said. 'Look closer. It's a snake. See? There's the mouth and the fangs.'

'Oh yeah. It kind of gives me the creeps. And it's

weird the way it was stuck down there in the tunnel wall. It looked like it was put there on purpose, but why would anyone do that? And who? The Vikings maybe? Your dad did mention that Vikings used the Poddle years ago.'

'Could be. But what I'm most curious about is that weird flash that made the grate fall out.'

'Yeah, what was that?' exclaimed Will.

'I thought it was just my imagination. Or that I'd knocked my head,' Ash said. 'But it really happened, didn't it?'

Just then Joe and Miss Keegan re-entered the room. Arthur quickly hid the pendant in the top pocket of his pyjamas.

'Let's go home,' Joe said.

Joe had taken a half day from work and now drove Ash and Arthur home. Miss Keegan gave Will a lift; when the three had gone missing, the class had been dismissed early for the day, she'd explained.

When they reached their estate, Ash ran into her house; only Stace and Max were home this early and both were very confused to see their sister wearing flannel pyjamas and carrying her soaking school uniform in a plastic bag.

When Arthur got home, he put his uniform straight in the wash and went to go upstairs to change.

'One second, young man,' said Joe sternly. Arthur came back to him, shuffling his feet sheepishly. 'I'm glad you're safe. But don't ever do anything stupid like that ever again, do you hear me?' His face wore a stony, stern expression.

'I'm sorry, Dad.'

His face softened. 'Promise me you won't do anything like that again. I've lost enough this year without losing you too.' They closed their arms around each other in a tight hug, both grateful that they were still alive to do it.

As Arthur slept that night, the pendant sat on his

bedside table. He turned over in his sleep, groaning. If he'd been awake, he would have seen the pendant start to glow. An eerie green light emanated from the bronze medal. But Arthur was trapped in a nightmare, dreaming of dark tunnels and letters he couldn't understand and hissing, hidden monsters.

CHAPTER EIGHT

Wednesday morning came and, as usual, Ash was waiting in Arthur's driveway when he left his house. She held something out to him. He took the gift from her: it was a brown leather shoelace.

'What's this for?'

'For the pendant. I'm guessing you have it with you? It's so you won't lose it.'

He did indeed have the pendant in his pocket. He took it out, threaded the lace through the loop at the top and tied it around his neck. He stuffed the pendant inside his shirt, where it felt momentarily cold against his bare chest.

'Thanks,' he said. 'Where'd you get it?'

'An old pair of my dad's shoes. It's all right, though – he never wears them. He's more of a Nike man.'

Cheerfully they made their way to school.

When they got there, there was no sign of Miss Keegan, but Will was surrounded by the class and was right in the middle of recounting their adventure of the previous day. He'd replaced the hospital bandage with a smaller Band-Aid and the cut over his eye seemed to be healing nicely. Their classmates listened in rapt silence to his every word.

'And it stank so bad down there. I didn't see any rats, but I'm sure there were loads. And –'

'Skip to the good part,' encouraged Rob Tynan. 'Tell us about when it flooded.'

'Well, the tide just started coming in real suddenly, right. This wave came out of nowhere, down the tunnel and,' he slapped the desk he was standing at, '*smashed* right into us. It knocked us all off our feet. It hit me so hard that I slammed my head on the ground.' He rubbed the Band-Aid over his eyebrow where it still stung. He saw Arthur and Ash enter behind the kids crowded around him. 'But, eh, I was lucky. Because

Arthur saw me in the water and helped me. He saved me.'

The class turned to Arthur. A few congratulated him, while others patted him on the back.

'What happened then?' prompted Rob.

'What happened then is that their lovely teacher came in and it was time to start class,' Miss Keegan said as she entered the room. 'Everyone take your seats, please. I'm sure there'll be lots of time to talk to our three adventurers during the break.' The pupils hustled to their desks, chair legs screeching on the floor. 'Settle down, settle down. Now, before Arthur, Will and Ashling decided to go for a little swim yesterday, we did actually have a very interesting and informative tour thanks to Arthur's father. So I'd like you all to spend the next, say, two hours writing an essay on what you learned about the new Metro. You can include pictures if you want. You can focus on one aspect of the Metro or on the whole thing. You can write about the excavation or write about what it'll mean to the city when it's complete. It's totally up to you. You can begin.'

She looked at her watch and sat down to correct the previous Monday's maths homework. Arthur decided to focus on the work that his father was doing at the Metro – he'd bring in all of Joe's past tunnelling experience as well as how the Usher's Quay tunnel would eventually be constructed. He might even touch on how the Metro would be joining the east of the city to the west. But one thing he would certainly not be writing about was the River Poddle. He suspected that neither Ash nor Will would want to revisit that particular topic either.

When the two hours were up, it was time for break. The school bell rang and the class filed out; everyone handing their essay to Miss Keegan as they passed. Arthur handed his up and was just pushing out the door with Ash and Will when Miss Keegan called him back.

She was looking at his essay as she leaned against her desk.

'Miss Keegan?'

'Take a seat please, Arthur.' He sat down in the front row before her. She noticed Ash and Will standing in the doorway, waiting for him. 'Out, you two! He'll follow you.' Casting a quizzical look towards Arthur, they walked off, leaving Arthur alone with the teacher.

'Look, Arthur,' Miss Keegan sighed, 'I know yesterday was a hard day for you. I'm sure you're still a bit shaky after your ordeal.'

'Well, a little, yes.'

'But I did ask you to do some work. Will and Ash managed to do theirs. Why couldn't you do yours?'

'Miss? I don't know what you mean.'

'The essay, Arthur. Why didn't you write an essay like everyone else in class?'

'But I did, Miss.' And he had. He'd put a lot of work into that essay for the past couple of hours. He could even remember the last line about how the Metro would be great for tourism.

'Arthur, please. You spent two hours doodling.' She held up his essay. His name was written on the top, like he remembered doing. And the first few lines of the essay were still intact. But after line five, his writing disintegrated into random lines, dots and cross-hatches. He took the pages from her and flicked through them, confused. Page after page was the same – an identical pattern repeated over and over in place of real letters.

'I can't … I didn't …' He struggled to continue. He knew two things as he looked at the pages. First of all, he definitely hadn't drawn these strange letters. He distinctly remembered writing the essay. But these *were* his pages, which just made him more confused.

The second thing he knew was that he'd seen these letters before. Carved into the wall of the stone tunnel and written in blood in a dream. An ancient alphabet that he shouldn't have, and couldn't have, known. Something called runes.

※※※※※

'And what did you say to her?' asked Ash. During break, Arthur had shown her and Will the pages. Will was currently studying them.

'I just apologised,' Arthur answered. 'I didn't know what else to say. She's letting me write the essay again for homework. I'm not worried about that, though. I'm worried that somebody must have swapped my essay for this.'

'You know what would be even worse, though?' said Will, looking up from the pages. 'That you did write this but you just can't remember doing it.'

'That's not possible,' Arthur said, then looked to Ash for confirmation. 'Is it?'

She shrugged her shoulders doubtfully and, though Arthur didn't want to admit it, he was doubtful too.

✸✸✸✸✸

Arthur didn't finish rewriting his essay that night until after 10.30. Exhausted, he went straight to bed. Joe followed to his own bed less than an hour later.

On the green outside, the dark figure emerged from the shadow of a tree and walked towards the Quinn household. Dead leaves crunched under his step while the breeze swept others around his ankles in mini typhoons.

He stopped in the middle of the road. This was far

enough. At this distance, he could sense the power of the pendant. He could even see it, glowing green through the boy's window as he dreamed inside.

The boy was protected now. Protected from him. Because of the pendant. Except it was more than a pendant. The man knew this. He knew what it really was. A key.

CHAPTER NINE

If Arthur thought that things couldn't get any stranger, he was in for a surprise the next day at school. Class was well under way. Miss Keegan had taken his new essay with thanks when he arrived in the door with Ash and Will, and on the board she was now going over some geography homework from a couple of days ago.

As she droned on about mounds and fjords and glacial formations, Arthur found himself being distracted by a strange smell. At first he couldn't tell what it was but as it grew stronger he found the smell in his memory. The air reeked of dampness and mildew, age and a faint whiff of open sewage. He'd smelled it before: under the ground, along the dank River Poddle. He looked at Ash and Will, but they didn't seem to have noticed and were both paying close attention to Miss Keegan's words on the blackboard. He looked at the teacher. Her mouth was moving and her hands gesturing yet suddenly he couldn't hear a word that was coming out. In fact, there was now total silence in the class. Total silence apart from a distant dripping sound. *Drip-drip-drip-drip*. It seemed to echo off the classroom walls.

Drip-drip-drip-drip.

He suddenly sensed something at his feet. He looked down to find that he was sitting in a boat. When he looked back up, he was no longer in the classroom, instead he was travelling down the River Poddle. The boat was narrow and basic, barely more than a raft really. The edges were curved inwards so that the water couldn't seep in. There was no one rowing or even steering; the little boat was being taken along by the flow of the water. It meandered down the river, walled on either side by a cold stone tunnel. A single torch burned, fixed to the bow.

Arthur sat in the stern. Even though he didn't know how long he'd been there or how he'd gotten there, and even though all he knew was that he was back in the dark Poddle tunnel on a small wooden raft, he wasn't frightened. But then he wasn't exactly calm either. He felt anxious, like there was an important task at hand that he had to carry out. He forgot all about his classroom, his friends and his teacher, and tried to remember what that task was.

The only sound now was the water lapping against the boat. No – that wasn't quite right. It was the sound of water lapping against boats, several boats. He turned around. For as far as he could see behind him, identical boats to his own followed. Each had its own torch, the light flickering on the stone walls and reflecting off the murky waters. But each boat had more than one passenger; in some as little as two, in others as many as five squeezed onto the fragile rafts. They were mostly men, although some looked as though they were barely out of boyhood, with long hair and beards, and were wearing dark tunics and heavy woollen shawls. Some of the men had weapons and shields with them in their boats; others had tools and building materials. Arthur looked down at his clothes and found that he was wearing a similar itchy tunic. He also had a few silver bracelets on his wrist and a necklace with the bronze pendant lying against his chest.

He scratched his head in confusion and found that his hair was long. It grew as far as his neckline and had a greasy, lanky feel to it. He rubbed his jaw to find a thick and bristly beard there. When he looked at his hands, he saw only a man's hands: veiny and thick with a fine layer of hair over the back.

Without really meaning to, he found himself reaching out to the wall to stop the boat. The others stopped behind him. He stood up, unsure of what he was doing but not in the least wobbly in the boat. His manly hands felt along the stone wall, finding the perfect spot. He pulled the pendant harshly and the necklace split, then he slammed the pendant against the wall. There was a brief green flash of light. When he took his hand away, the piece of bronze was embedded in the stone, glowing faintly. The light faded as he turned to speak to his army.

Strange, Arthur thought distantly, that I know they're an army.

The voice coming through Arthur's lips wasn't his own: it was a deep baritone, echoing off the tunnel walls. And it spoke in a language that Arthur couldn't understand. The men nodded agreement and he sat back down. The boat moved on by itself.

They travelled further down the river than Arthur, Will and Ash had explored. And yet, somehow he knew that what he was seeing was accurate. He knew that the scratches on the walls were real; he knew that the turn to the right they soon came across was authentic.

There was a light in the distance. It was flickering orange so Arthur knew it was firelight, but it was much brighter than the torches they had. As the boat moved closer, he realised he was looking through a door and into a large, cavernous room. Several torches adorned the wall he could see.

Then one torch in the room blinked out as they approached. It hadn't been blown out; it just looked like it had run out of fuel or oxygen. Another went dark, and another, and another, until the room through the door was pitch black.

He looked at his own torch, and as he did every torch on every boat faded to darkness.

※※※※※

'Aaah!'

Arthur opened his eyes and was shocked to find himself sitting in the middle of class. For a brief moment, he wasn't sure if he'd actually woken at all or was still dreaming. But the giggles coming from some class members gave it away.

'Am I boring you, Arthur?' Miss Keegan said. She was holding a piece of chalk in her hand, midway through writing some geography answers on the board.

'No, Miss, I'm sorry.'

'Glad to hear it. Now, may I continue?'

'Of course, Miss. Sorry, Miss.'

She turned back to the board and went on writing.

Will nudged him. 'Are you all right?'

Arthur nodded.

'Are you sure?' whispered Ash, concern written all over her face.

'Yeah. I just haven't been sleeping well. I keep having these weird dreams …'

He trailed off mid-sentence when he saw the words that Miss Keegan was writing on the board. The geography answers, which had been written in plain English, were moving by themselves across the board. The chalk letters looked like they were dancing.

'Hey! Look at that!'

'What?'

'That! Don't you see it?' He pointed to the blackboard where the letters continued to move independently. No one else seemed to notice; not Will, not Ash, not even Miss Keegan, who was writing more words on the board, only for them to come to life too. The letters suddenly slowed down and started to form new shapes: lines, x shapes, crosses, dots and crosshatching. All shapes similar to the ones he'd seen on the wall of the tunnel, shapes he'd somehow written down himself the day before.

Miss Keegan turned and noticed Arthur's boggled face watching the board. She opened her mouth to speak but the words that came out weren't English. Arthur didn't have to listen long to realise that she was speaking the strange foreign language he'd just heard in his dream.

He jumped off his chair in shock and fear, but became tangled in the strap of his backpack and fell to the floor. When Ash moved to help him up, speaking the same strange language, he recoiled from her. Will grabbed him by the forearm and helped him to his feet, also speaking in the dream dialogue.

Arthur snatched his arm away, ran for the door, through it and down the corridor. He didn't stop running until he was halfway home and his lungs felt like they were about to burst. He bent over and rested his hands on his knees, panting.

'It's a dream!' he kept muttering to himself. 'It's a dream, it's a dream! Just wake up!'

The pendant slipped out from under his shirt and dangled on its lace in front of his face. It was shimmering with a bright green light. He looked at it, pulled it off straight over his head and shoved it in his pocket. Then he ran the rest of the way home as quickly as he could.

※※※※

The doorbell rang just after four o'clock. Arthur answered it to find Ash and Will standing there. Will held up Arthur's backpack.

'You forgot this,' he said.

'Thanks. Am I in trouble?'

'Well, you could probably do with saying sorry to Miss Keegan.'

'I'll do that tomorrow. Come in.'

When Arthur had described everything that had happened in the classroom to them, he took the pendant out of his pocket and placed it on the kitchen table between them. It was still glowing faintly.

'How is it doing that?' Ash mused.

'I don't know,' Arthur said. 'It's definitely making me see things, hallucinate. And I think it's making me do things as well, like writing in those bizarre letters yesterday in the essay. On top of that, I had another strange dream a couple of weeks ago. I think they all may be linked somehow, but the pendant couldn't have given me that weird dream because we hadn't found it yet.'

'What happened in it?' asked Ash.

'It felt strange, different somehow. You know when you're in a dream, you're always living it? Well, in this one it felt like I was watching. And I saw this crazy-looking guy and a snake. Only the snake grew huge. And those letters were there as well. They were called runes.'

'But the pendant is still magic or something, right?' added Will. 'It's probably the reason you heard us speak that language. And why you saw the letters change on the blackboard.'

'It's a translator,' murmured Ash.

'What?'

'It's a translator. Some kind of magical translator. If you see or hear something in English, it gets turned into this odd ancient language.'

'Could be,' agreed Arthur. Another light bulb lit

up over his head. 'But what would happen if you saw something in the ancient language?'

'What are you getting at?' said Will. But Arthur was already running upstairs. He came back down a moment later, carrying the pages of his failed essay.

As he smoothed them out on the table, he explained. 'When I wrote these I was wearing the pendant. It translated them from English to this language but I didn't realise it. So maybe …'

He tentatively put the pendant back around his neck. Instantly the glowing became more intense.

At first nothing happened. But then the strange patterns on the page started to dance like they'd done on the blackboard. They moved and shifted across the page until finally settling.

'Anything?' Will asked, looking anxiously at the essay. 'What does it say?'

Arthur couldn't take his eyes from the pages, from the message he couldn't remember writing. A message he didn't understand.

'It says …' he began, 'it says the same thing over and over. The same three words. "Beware the Jormungand".'

He looked at his friends, fear in all their eyes.

'What's a Jormungand?' Ash said.

'I'm not sure,' Arthur replied, 'but I'm really worried.'

'Why?'

'Well, because I think that might be what the crazy-looking guy called the giant snake thing in my dream, and if it is we're in really big trouble.'

CHAPTER TEN

The next day Arthur got the bus to school early by himself. Rather than wearing the pendant, he took it with him in his pocket for safety's sake. When he got to school, he waited outside their classroom, checking his watch nervously every few seconds. At this time of the morning, only the school caretaker strolled up and down the hall, sweeping and mopping the floor for the day ahead. Eventually, Miss Keegan rounded a corner and walked towards him.

'Arthur?' she said when she reached him. 'You're here very early.'

'Miss Keegan, I just want to say I'm sorry. For yesterday.'

'It really was unacceptable, Arthur.' She turned the key in the classroom door and went in. Arthur followed her inside. She put down her bag, sat on the edge of her desk and crossed her arms.

'Look,' she said, 'I know you're having a hard time, what with moving to Dublin so suddenly and almost drowning the other day. But I can't cover for you again. Do you have any idea how much trouble I was in after that?'

Arthur looked down bashfully at his shuffling feet. 'No, Miss.'

'A lot. Thankfully your parents all understood. But next time there's an incident like this, it'll be up to you to explain to the principal and your father.'

'Yes, Miss. I'm sorry, Miss. It won't happen again.'

'It had better not. Anyway, apology accepted.' The school bell chimed. 'You may as well take your seat. Class will be starting in a few minutes.'

A short time later, everyone else bustled into the classroom and Ash and Will sat next to him.

'Where were you this morning?' Ash asked.

'Apologising.'

'Well, we have some news about your Jormungand,' Will said. 'Ash found –'

'When you're finished talking, Will, we'll begin the class,' Miss Keegan interrupted.

'Sorry, Miss.'

'Thank you.' She addressed the class then. 'Now, I really enjoyed marking your essays. And you all clearly enjoyed writing them.' She walked through the room, handing back the corrected pages. 'So you can use them as the basis for your weekend homework.'

There was a groan at the phrase 'weekend homework'.

'Come on,' she said with a chuckle, 'you'll have fun with this. I want you to get into groups of two. Each group will give a presentation to the class on Monday about the Metro. You can all expand on what you've written already. I'd like each group to try and discover something new that we didn't know before. You could find out about the history of tunnelling or you could research other underground train systems. Whatever. Just enjoy yourselves. So for the first hour this morning, I'd like you all to get into groups and discuss what you're going to do.'

It was quickly decided that Arthur and Ash should be one group as they lived so close to each other. Will paired up with Rob Tynan and moved to his desk to decide what they'd do their presentation on.

'So?' Arthur said to Ash. 'What did you have to tell me?'

'Stace wants to be an actress, right? And last summer she applied for work experience at this place.'

Ash took a folded-up piece of paper from her bag and slid it across the desk to him. He opened it out: it was a glossy flyer.

'She didn't get the job,' Ash continued, 'but she still had the flyer when I, um, borrowed it from her room last night.'

In bold Celtic text across the top, it read 'Viking Experience'. Underneath that was a photo of a recreated Viking village. The houses were made out of plywood but painted to look like they'd been constructed from stone. They had thatched roofs and some loose straw lay on the cobbled ground. A couple of farm animals were locked up in basic-looking barns, while some people dressed in Viking costumes

– mainly long, drab, woollen tunics – went about their business. One Viking faced the camera, with his hands on his hips. He was wearing a brighter-coloured cape with a brooch pinning it into place and a silver crown on his head. A speech bubble came out of his mouth: 'Come along to the Viking Experience and see how Vikings really lived in ancient Dublin! Learn our customs and our legends!' At the bottom of the flyer was the Viking Experience website address, pricing, opening times and location information.

'You think we should go here and find out what exactly?' he asked, passing her back the flyer.

She slid it back to him again. 'Look at his brooch.'

Because of the high-gloss paper, Arthur had to squint to make out the image on the brooch. But there was no doubting what it was. Although not as intricate as the design on his pendant, the brooch definitely showed a snake coiled around a tree trunk.

'Wow!' he exclaimed. 'Well spotted, Ash.'

'Tomorrow's Saturday. So the three of us can get the bus into town. The Viking Experience is actually quite close to the Metro site.'

'Perfect,' he said. 'Tomorrow it is.'

Arthur knocked at Ash's front door the following morning. Max answered in full football kit including jersey, shorts and socks that came up to and over his knees. As usual, he was holding a football.

'Are you coming to play with me, Arthur?' He was already running down the drive when Arthur called him back.

'Sorry, Max,' he said. 'Me and Ash are going into town.'

Ash came out of the house, zipping up her warm jacket.

'And you're not invited,' she added.

'Why not?' Max demanded in disgust.

'Just 'cos,' Ash said. 'Now go back inside: you'll freeze in those shorts.'

'No fair!' sulked Max as Arthur and Ash walked in the direction of the bus stop.

They'd arranged to meet Will at the bus shelter at

eleven o'clock, and he was already waiting when they got there. They didn't have to hang around too long before a bus pulled up. They boarded and made their way into town.

As was always the case for a Saturday morning in Dublin, traffic was heavy so it took them longer than expected to get to the Viking Experience. A year ago the large, open square area in the Smithfield district of Dublin had been bare. Then a bright spark in the council suggested erecting the Viking Experience there. The cobbled paving stones made it the perfect location and it was sure to bring more tourism to Smithfield itself. So the fake village was built, surrounded by a tall brick wall covered in Viking-themed murals and ivy.

To enter the Viking Experience, they had to cross a little wooden bridge over an artificial moat. A sentry in full Viking costume stood at the gate, nodding grimly to people as they went in when he wasn't texting on his phone.

'How's it goin', man?' Will said to him as they passed. The phoney Viking scowled, not at all impressed.

Just beyond the gate was a small room with a ticket booth. The teenage girl behind the Perspex window was wearing a gold-coloured crown and chewing gum.

'That'll be four silver coins for each squire or young lady,' she said half-heartedly.

'Huh?' Arthur said.

'Four euro each for children,' she translated. She took the money from them and handed them their tickets. 'Just wait over there and your tour guide will be with you in a minute.'

They joined a group of chattering, excited tourists. Many had cameras around their necks in anticipation of the photo opportunities the flyer promised, while others were reading the guide book that you could purchase for a nominal fee.

'I don't know how much we're going to learn here,' Arthur said doubtfully.

Suddenly, a man bounded through a door behind the ticket booth. They recognised him instantly as the Viking on the flyer. He was even wearing the same costume, complete with the replica brooch. He drew himself up in front of the group, as if he was a king surveying his subjects.

'Welcome!' he said in a laboured British accent. 'Welcome, travellers from the future. My name is Olaf Cuaran. The year is AD 945 and I am the Viking king of this city of Dyflin – though I believe you prefer to call it Dublin.' As he spoke, he gestured theatrically, waving his arms to every beat in the sentence. 'Where are my manners?' he continued, putting his hand on his chest in mock shock. 'Would you like to see the city?'

Some of the tour group played along and murmured that they would indeed like to see the city. The actor playing Olaf turned to a door and pushed it open.

'This way, please, future-travellers.'

Will whispered to Arthur and Ash, 'Why is he speaking in a British accent? The Vikings were Scandinavian.'

Olaf heard him and turned. 'It's more regal, and anyway, I can't do Scandinavian,' he said through gritted teeth.

He pushed the door open and led them into the

replica city, although city was a very loose term for the random scattering of houses and barns that made up the Viking Experience. It was just as they'd seen in the flyer. Actors in Viking costumes moved about as if they didn't even notice the tour group. Some pushed carts piled high with hay; others carried loaves of hard bread to a market somewhere; still more tended to animals in the makeshift barns. There was a heady aroma of burning wood, which Arthur recognised from Bonfire Night back in Kerry, and some medieval music playing from a few discreetly hidden speakers positioned throughout the village.

Olaf continued his speech as he guided the group through the small streets. 'We Vikings settled here many years ago, in AD 841. Dublin is a very important Viking trading town. Ships come from all over the known world and trade with us here. We trade in meat, spices, herbs and even slaves. But trade is why we settled on a city where two rivers meet in the centre: the Liffey and the Poddle.' He stopped and indicated the cobblestones they were walking on. 'Nowadays, the Poddle runs underground and it's from where this river and the Liffey meet that Dublin gets its name: the Black Pool, or Dubh Linn.'

Some tourists snapped photos of the straw-littered cobblestones.

'This way, please,' Olaf carried on, leading them down a narrow street. It was so narrow, in fact, that they had to walk in single file between the buildings. They were able to look directly through the front doors of all the houses. Mannequins dressed in Viking costumes were arranged inside to represent real people. They were cooking, laughing, playing, feeding babies. Arthur could tell that they'd been used in other museums and displays before, as the paint on their waxy faces was cracked and peeling and had grown discoloured over time. The houses were basic: ten-foot square, four walls, no windows and only one room in each. Some of the houses had real wood-burning fires set up in the centre of the floor; the smoke escaped through a hole cut into the thatched roof.

'You can see how my subjects live,' Olaf said, looking into the shacks. 'It's basic accommodation but they're happy. However, we Vikings are not very clean – and certainly not environmentally friendly.' He made quotation marks with his fingers as he said this, then drew their attention to the huge piles of rubbish and waste food dropped outside each house. There was no smell, so Arthur assumed the rotting food was just a prop.

They came out into a small, open square area. There was a barn on either side containing both real and fibreglass animals. Ahead of them was a little market with stalls set up, selling and trading food, building materials, animals and clothes. Actors wandered through the market at a leisurely pace, smiling and joking with each other.

King Olaf stopped in the centre of the square. 'In the market behind me, you can find anything a Viking might need: meat, butter, even wool for clothes.' He studied the tour group closely. 'I see a lot of you are wearing trousers. Did you know that we Vikings introduced trousers to Ireland? And I suppose you're wondering why I'm not wearing a horned helmet? Well, you see we Vikings never wore horns on our helmets – although we are skilled craftsmen, famous for our weaponry and jewellery.'

Arthur saw Ash raising her hand. Olaf saw it too.

'We usually leave questions till the end, young traveller,' he said.

'I was just wondering, though,' she started, 'if you could tell us about that brooch you're wearing?'

'This brooch?' he said, looking down at the replica pinned to his cape.

'Yes. What does it mean – the snake wrapped around the tree?'

'Ah, well that's the sign of the Jormungand.'

'The what?' Arthur cried out.

Olaf rolled his eyes, clearly irritated. 'Well, I guess we're having questions now instead,' he muttered to himself in his natural Irish accent.

'The brooch depicts the Jormungand,' he said, back in character. 'I wear this because it protects me from the evil god Loki.'

Loki! Arthur recalled now that that was the name of the man in his dream a couple of weeks ago.

'Did somebody say "*Loki*"?' a high-pitched voice cried from the side of one of the barns. Another actor emerged, wearing a cheap-looking long, straggly blond wig and beard. He had a bright green tunic on and yellow trousers underneath, stained at the ankles. He bounded across the cobbles to join Olaf.

'Is *that* supposed to be Loki?' Will asked derisively.

'I *am* Loki!' the new actor insisted.

'Loki is a trickster god,' Olaf explained. 'He's mischievous, a liar. Don't trust him. Although you can get your photo taken with him at the end of the tour should you wish. Loki, I was just about to tell our guests the story of the Jormungand. Do you want to have the honour?'

'My pleasure!'

Loki walked through the crowd as he told the story, playfully knocking caps off tourists' heads or making funny faces at the children.

'For hundreds of years,' he said, 'I played tricks on humans and on the other gods. I'd make a pregnant woman give birth to a pig just to see her face. Or I'd give a cow sharp teeth so that she could eat her farmer instead. So funny. So very, very *funny*.' He rubbed Arthur's head patronisingly as he passed. 'But after a while I got bored of that. So I created my three children. And the first one was the Jormungand.'

Olaf spoke up here. 'The Jormungand was a giant snake. It's also known as the Midgard Serpent or the World Serpent. It was said that it could eat the world piece by piece till nothing was left. That's why it's always depicted strangling a tree: the tree of life.'

'But it didn't work!' shouted Loki. 'It didn't work!' He started crying loudly then suddenly ran into the market. He knocked over a stall as he went and laughed wildly. Arthur thought he probably should have won an Oscar for that demented performance. Or at least that he probably wanted to win an Oscar.

'Anyway, let's continue our tour,' said Olaf.

'Wait,' Arthur said. 'What did he mean "it didn't work"?'

Olaf sighed heavily. 'Okay. Thor, son of the good god Odin, led a battle against the Jormungand. The battle ended at the edge of the world and Thor managed to defeat the beast but the great warrior took only nine steps from the fallen serpent before he died himself. The serpent wasn't killed, but it was so tired from the battle that it fell into an eternal sleep. The Vikings buried the Jormungand underground, along with a hundred men to guard it. Now, shall we continue our tour? This way, please.'

'What happened then?' Ash asked.

'Look, kid,' Olaf started, totally out of character by this stage and approaching Ash angrily, 'it doesn't matter, all right! It's just a story. Now, please, we have to finish the tour soon, so let's hustle.'

As Olaf herded the group through the market, Arthur, Will and Ash fell back.

'What do you think?' Arthur said.

'I don't know what to make of it all,' answered Will.

'What do you think, Arthur?' Ash asked.

'I'm thinking …' he started. He didn't want to finish the thought but knew he had to. 'I'm thinking that I saw Loki create the Jormungand in a dream. And I'm thinking that … that it's not just a story.'

'In that case, I think we should go back,' said Will.

'What do you mean "go back"?' Arthur asked. 'Back home?'

'No. To the tunnel, to the River Poddle.'

'Why would we do that?' asked Ash, shocked.

'Well, something is clearly happening – it can't be a coincidence that Arthur is suddenly having these weird dreams about the Jormungand and Loki and the Poddle and that we found the pendant in the Poddle tunnel. We need to go back to see what else we find. There might be more pendants down there. Or some clues about what's going on. Or –'

'No,' Arthur interrupted, 'we're not going back. It's too dangerous.' He looked back at the market where the fake Loki was running amok through the stalls. 'Anyway, the Loki in my dream was way scarier than that guy. I don't want to take any chances.'

CHAPTER ELEVEN

In a time before written history, in Asgard, the realm of the gods, there is a great spring named the Well of Urd. This reservoir contains all the knowledge of all the worlds that is, that was and that will be. As such, the Well of Urd is bottomless, as new wisdom forms every second of every minute of every day.

Though picturesque, the well doesn't look like much at first glance. It appears to be little more than a pond, barely large enough for two swans to spread their wings, with rocks forming a small wall around the edge. It is hidden away at the outer boundary of a forest, against a high cliff. Water pours down the cliff wall from an unseen river above and into the well, foaming as it crashes against the larger rocks. The water isn't clear – it's murky, filled with dust and weeds and white froth. No man could hope to gain knowledge from these dark waters by himself.

Every day, the twelve gods and twelve goddesses who reside in Asgard come to the well. They come not to stare into the cloudy water but to seek counsel from the keepers of the well. The three keepers are known as the Norns: Urd, Skuld and Verdandi.

Wind and rain lash the plains of Asgard this morning, a bad omen. The gods travel on chariots led by pigs and goats through the woods. None of them wears their battle helmet today, only capes with hoods to protect themselves from the raindrops. Odin stands out from the rest. He rides ahead on a great steed. He wears a wide-brimmed, brown leather hat which casts half his face in shadow. His right eye is gone and a leather patch covers the gaping hole. He traded the eye centuries ago in return for great knowledge and yet even he must bow to the wisdom of the three Norns. He is the leader of the gods, known as the All Father, the Battle God and One-Eyed. And today he seeks answers more urgently than ever before. Today, one of the gods is missing. Loki.

When they reach the Well of Urd, the All Father climbs down from his horse, walks to the spring and dips his fingers into the bubbling water. It is icy cold. He looks into the well and sees only darkness. The three Norns are nowhere to be seen. He shakes the drops from his hand and takes a couple of steps backwards. The other gods and goddesses watch him in silence.

He breathes deeply then speaks. 'I, Odin All Father, the one-eyed god of battle, the ruler of Asgard, come here to seek counsel with the three ageless Norns. Behind me are the gods and goddesses of Asgard, all save one, and we implore you to speak to us.'

They all hold their breath, watching the foaming waterfall for any sign of movement.

'We beg of you, oh great and wise Norns, come and grant us your counsel.'

Then something happens. Three figures step forward from behind the waterfall, from out of the rocky cliff wall. They stop directly under the water, where their features are hidden by the foaming shower. The gods can only make out impressions of the figures: they are all female, with long hair slicked to their heads by the moisture, they are slender and they stand impossibly still. As the water runs over their faces, the gods can just about see the hollows of their eyes. These are the Norns: older than the gods, older than time itself. Only they can read the knowledge in the well, only they know the truth of fate, the present and the future.

'We are here, Odin All Father,' they say in three voices as one. 'What answers do you seek?'

Odin takes a step forward. He takes off his hat, exposing his balding head to the rain.

'Thank you,' he says. 'We come seeking answers about one of our own. For the past three days and nights, none of us has seen or heard from the Father of Lies, Loki. We have asked the birds in the skies and the fish in the seas to look for him, but none can locate him. Surely this is a trick of his, but we need to find him. And we need to know what he's doing.'

Verdandi, the Norn on the left, looks deep into the

well. She can read all that the waters can tell her about the present.

After a time, she looks back at Odin and speaks. 'The one you seek, Loki, is in the east. It is true that he tricked the birds of the skies and the fish of the seas so that they could not find him. He is content now, but he has not been for some time. He felt anger at you, Odin All Father, and the other gods of Asgard. He felt shame and disgust and he blames you all. He swore vengeance.'

At this, the gods gasp and start protesting loudly. Odin tries to quiet them, but they persist.

'Do you wish for me to continue?' asks Verdandi.

'Please,' says Odin. Then he turns to the other gods, commanding, 'Be quiet all of you. We have more to learn.'

At this they grow silent and Verdandi continues. 'Loki swore vengeance. And so, the Father of Lies became a father himself. He has created three children. These children, his evil brood, have one purpose in mind: to destroy all of creation.'

Again, the gods break into a loud, worried

discussion. Odin silences them with a glare and turns back to the Norn.

'That is all I have to say,' Verdandi intones. 'My sisters may have more to tell you, Odin All Father.'

'Thank you.' Odin bows his head. 'Skuld, perhaps you can tell me how to stop this madness?'

Skuld, the Norn on the right, tilts her head and stares into the well. She can see all of the near future.

Eventually she looks up at the gods and begins. 'To stop Loki's evil brood, you must send your greatest warriors, Odin All Father, and they should be led by your own son, Thor. It will be a battle that you will win but, I warn you, a high price will be paid. You must not allow Loki to use his power in this way again.'

'We will apologise to Loki then,' Odin says, 'to appease him.'

'No. The time for that is past. You must bind him. It would do no good to lock him in your prisons. And you cannot kill him, because it is a terrible thing for one god to kill another. If a god kills another, their purity dies. They will become evil – as bad as Loki himself.'

'Then what should we do? How should we bind him?'

'His mind and his tongue are his greatest weapons. You cannot allow him to use these. When you capture him, take him to the end of the world. There is a cave there underneath a small settlement whose men are loyal to you. You must do all that you can to dull his mind. If his mind is sharp, he will be able to use it to think of escape. Do not allow this to happen. That is all I have to say. Perhaps my sister can tell you more.'

Without even a prompt from Odin, the Norn in the centre looks into the water. This is Urd, the eldest Norn, and the well is named after her. She is also the most mysterious, knowing all there is about fate and destiny. After staring into the depths for longer than her sisters, she looks to Odin.

'Odin All Father,' she says, 'you must trust me that what I tell you now is all that I can tell you, for no man or god must know too much of his fate. Do you understand?'

'I understand.'

'Good. Then I'll begin.' Urd nods. 'In the far future, Loki will escape.'

There is a collective gasp from the surrounding

151

gods. Even Odin seems taken aback. Urd continues to speak.

'Though I can't say how, he will escape his binding. He will try to start again what he is attempting to do now. If he succeeds in this future time, then the outcome will be grave. Even for us Norns. By unleashing his brood upon the world a second time, he will start Ragnarok.'

The anxious chatter of the gods grows louder again. Odin shouts over them. 'How can we stop him in the future?'

'You can't,' answers Urd grimly. 'You will want to but you can't. You must merely watch. There is only one who might be able to stop him. A boy. A young boy and his friends. One of them is watching us right now.'

'What?' exclaims Odin, looking around fearfully. 'Where?'

'Right there,' Urd says, and her ghostly arm raises and points out of the waterfall towards –

Arthur woke in a panic when the crazy waterfall woman pointed at him. The sky was growing bright outside his window he realised as he sat up in bed. He checked the time on his watch: just after six in the morning. Too early to give Ash or Will a call anyway.

He dropped the watch back on his bedside table and rubbed the sleep out of his eyes furiously, thinking back on the dream. But was it a dream? Or was it another vision? Some kind of link to the past and another world? He looked at the pendant on his bedside locker. It wasn't glowing even slightly, so it didn't seem to Arthur like it was causing these strange dreams about the gods. Gods he'd never even heard of until they'd moved to Dublin.

He leaped out of bed and ran to his desk where he pulled a blank sheet of paper from a copybook and started writing. He didn't want to forget anything he'd seen or heard in the dream and decided to note everything down before it faded from his memory the way details from the first one had:

Odin – All Father – good

Gods – good

Loki – Father of Lies – bad

Thor – Odin's son – goes to fight Loki's children

Norns – Some kind of weird fortune-tellers, Urd, Skuld
and Verdandi

Asgard – Where the gods live

To this list he then added:

Jormungand – Loki's first child (he had three) – giant
snake – 'World Serpent'

When he was done, he appraised the list. It was still all a big mystery to him. Too big. Without realising it, he was rubbing the ribbon on his wrist. He looked down at it and thought of his mother. She would have known what to do, or if not she would have tried to help him. She'd always been interested in mythology, encouraged him to read the legends of other places and times, but he had always put it off. If only he'd taken her advice ... As he sat there alone in his room, he wanted to cry but found he couldn't.

CHAPTER TWELVE

Arthur didn't sleep after that. He spent the early hours of the morning pacing the house, going over everything in his mind. He eventually sat down and made himself eat breakfast around nine. He quickly swallowed a bowl of Rice Krispies, then threw on some clothes and raced over to Ash's house.

Ash was still in her dressing gown when she answered the door.

'Morning, Arthur. What has you up so early?'

'I have some stuff to tell you. Some Viking stuff. Can I come in?'

Ash led him into the living room where, over the next ten minutes, he recounted in as much detail as he could his dream of the Norns. When he was done, she stared into the distance for a few seconds before speaking.

'Wow,' she said. 'Well, we learned a lot there.'

'Did we?' he said doubtfully. 'Like what?'

'Now we know that the gods managed to stop Loki before, but that he must have got out of his prison somehow, just like Urd foretold.'

'I guess. Then there was that last thing she said …' He didn't really like thinking about the Norn pointing at him, saying that only a young boy and his friends could stop Loki.

'Exactly. Do you think she meant you?'

'I don't know. I don't like to think about it. I wish I could remember exactly what they said would happen when Loki returns this time. I just know it was bad.'

'Yeah. Real bad. Worse than forgetting your home-work or some –' As Ash spoke, she suddenly remembered that they still hadn't done any work on the presentation for school. 'Arthur! The presentation!'

For a moment his eyes were glazed in confusion. Then the realisation hit him like a ton of bricks. 'Oh no!'

For now, this homework was definitely more important than ancient monsters and evil gods. Ash leaped off her seat, saying she'd have to wash and dress before they started, and asked Arthur to wait in the kitchen. Arthur did as she said and found Ash's mother – a warm, bubbly woman in her late forties – in the kitchen fixing breakfast. After the introductions were done, she made Arthur some toast (with real butter and marmalade). Ash soon came back down wearing a pair of jeans, a T-shirt and a hoodie. Just as Arthur was about to take another bite of toast, Ash grabbed his hand and dragged him out the back door. She led him across the small, neatly kept garden.

'Where are we –?'

'I have the perfect idea!' she explained when they reached the small wooden shed at the end of her back garden. 'I thought of it when I was getting dressed.'

The shed door squeaked when she pulled it open. Inside, shelves were piled high with old paint cans and tins of oil. A large spider ambled across its web towards the carcass of a fly. Dust hung in the air, caught in the rays of light coming through the little square window. Some paintbrushes sat in a jar of murky white spirits, the paint long caked into the bristles. A few gardening tools – a rake, a hoe and a shovel – had fallen onto the electric lawnmower in the corner. And a wooden stepladder leaned on its side against the opposite wall.

'Give me a hand with this, will you?' she said, taking one end of the ladder.

It wasn't as heavy as it looked; it was just an awkward shape to lift single-handed. As they carried it into the house, Ash explained further.

'Miss Keegan loves it when you do something a bit unusual for class presentations. Like, if you're studying Ancient Rome, you'd dress up as Romans. In last year's class they were reading *The Wind in the Willows* and somebody brought in their pet toad. She loves stuff like that.'

They made their way through the kitchen, past a quizzical Mrs Barry and up the stairs with the ladder. Getting it through the stairwell was tricky and they had to reposition themselves a few times to manage it.

'So you're saying we dress up … as what?' Arthur

said as they opened the ladder under an attic door in the ceiling. 'Metro drivers?'

'No,' she said, mounting the ladder, 'I've an even better idea.' She pushed open the hatch and clambered into the attic. Then she looked back down at Arthur waiting on the landing. 'Are you coming or not?'

'The last time I followed someone on a ladder it didn't end very well, remember?' he joked, climbing up. There was a little round window in the gable wall of the attic. Dust danced in the light shafts that poured in through it. The roof was low enough for Arthur to reach up and touch the rafters, but not low enough that he had to stoop to walk around. There was an old moth-eaten mattress, turned on its side, and a lot of cardboard boxes cluttered together against one wall. Ash was searching through one such box with 'Toys' written on it in black marker.

'What are you looking for?' he asked.

She ignored him and lifted the box she'd been looking through to one side with a sigh. She dragged out another box, also marked 'Toys', and searched through it, throwing old dolls and action figures behind her as she did.

'Ash? What are you looking for?'

'Yes!' she exclaimed, finding what she needed, then turned back to Arthur. 'Sorry. Anyway, I was saying that Miss Keegan likes it when we do something more interesting for her presentations. Thinking outside the box. So I thought to myself, what's the best way to present the Metro to the class?'

'I don't know,' he said, as if she was telling a joke. 'What *is* the best way to present the Metro to the class?'

She took a toy train out of the box and held it up to him. 'We build one.'

※※※※※

Ash's idea was ingenious. Instead of just talking about the Metro trains and how they would run, they'd make a working scale model. Max's old train set was perfect. The electronics didn't work any more but Ash was confident that she'd be able to fix them given a couple of hours.

'It's a very simple circuit board,' she'd said. 'If I had more time I could probably make it run faster than the actual Metro.'

'Well, if you get it running at all, that's all we need,' Arthur had said with a laugh.

While she worked on the electronics, Arthur worked on making the toy look more like the new Metro trains. The toy train was shaped like an old steam engine whereas the Metro trains were going to be slick, silver and streamlined, with the Citi-Trak logo printed on the side. Ash had given him some light card, construction paper, scissors and markers and he set to work. Using images from the Citi-Trak website, he made a sort of hood that could be fitted straight over the toy engine, giving it the shape and look of the Metro trains. When he was finished with that, he set about making signs to indicate the different stops along the line.

As he worked, Ash kept stealing glances at him. She liked Arthur. A lot. In fact, she found herself liking this boy more than any other boy she knew. Something about him just made her smile. In fact, she was grinning like an idiot when he looked up and caught her.

'What are you smiling at?' he asked.

'Oh … eh …' she blustered and looked away shyly, then held up the train. 'I'm finished. Have a look at this.' She put the toy train on a one-metre length of track she'd assembled on the kitchen table. It sat idly there for a second before she pressed a button on the remote attached to the track. The train shot off at high speed, so fast, in fact, that it flew off the track and over the edge of the table.

'Well done!' Arthur patted her on the back.

'It was no big deal,' she said modestly, 'but we do need some more track.' She pointed to the length on the table. 'That's all I could find in the attic.'

'Where can we get some?'

'Shopping trip to town, I guess.'

'Can I come?' a voice said from behind the kitchen door. It was Max.

'What are you doing there?' said Ash. She hoped he hadn't seen the looks she'd been giving Arthur. 'And, more to the point, how long have you been hiding?'

'A while. Can I come? I'm bored. Stace and Mom are gone out. And Dad's watching one of his silly *Carry On* movies. Can I come, *please*?'

'No, you can't come.'

'Why not? You're using my train.'

'It's for a school project,' Ash said, putting on her coat. 'Now go and watch the movie with Dad. You don't really want to come. It'll be boring.'

'But …' he whined as Arthur and Ash walked out the door, laughing to themselves.

'What's more boring than a toyshop!' Arthur chuckled when they were out of earshot.

❋❋❋❋❋

When they got into the city centre, they went straight to the nearest and largest toyshop. Toyz Toyz Toyz consisted of three storeys where they could find any type of plaything they could possibly want. The pink teddy bear on the sign outside promised 'Magic and Fun under One Roof!' The ground floor consisted of baby and infant toys, a nursery section, video games, arts and crafts and board games. The first floor housed all the girls' toys and was wall to wall pink, cerise and magenta with baby dolls, dress-up sets and fashion-model heads. The top floor was mainly boys' toys: action figures, racing cars and construction sets, along with large outdoor toys like bikes, go-karts and playhouses.

They quickly found the extra pieces of train track they needed somewhere between the third aisle of infant toys and the first aisle of arts and crafts. Arthur gave Ash his half of the money for it and she went to pay.

'I'm just going for a wander,' he said and made his way up the escalators to the top floor. He wanted to take a look at the bicycles. Getting around Dublin was a lot harder than he'd thought it would be. Certainly much harder than at home, where he could just walk anywhere he wanted to go. He'd left his own bike in his grandparents' house in Kerry for safe-keeping but now he regretted it. He figured a bike in Dublin would probably come in handy.

When he got to the top floor, he was surprised to

find it so quiet. The other departments had been busy, with children, parents and staff bustling about. But up here it wasn't just quiet, it was completely deserted. Even the pop music that had been playing downstairs was switched off. It was like a ghost town.

Weird, he thought, before spotting the bike section past a long aisle of action figures. He ran towards it, his footsteps echoing on the blue linoleum floor. If Arthur had been more careful, he might have noticed that all the security cameras were pointing away from him and in towards the walls.

The bikes were displayed on a wall of racks. Most were black, though some were silver, but Arthur's eyes were instantly drawn to the glossy red ten-speed at one end of the display. He checked out the price. It was at least double his savings. In his head he did some basic maths, working out whether he could somehow find the necessary money. As he added and multiplied silently, he became gradually aware of a noise coming from behind the bike racks.

It sounded like a voice, like somebody speaking, maybe. No, not speaking, singing. He couldn't make out what, but it definitely was singing. Slowly but steadily he walked back along the aisle, his soles squeaking slightly on the lino as he went. The singing grew louder and eventually clearer as he turned the corner at the end of the racks, where playhouses, swings and slides were displayed. Because of the hollow, echoing sound of the singing, he assumed that it was coming from inside a large pink plastic playhouse in the centre of the display.

'Rock-a-bye baby on the tree top …'

The playhouse was designed like a princess's castle, with two turrets and a couple of bluebirds stuck to the roof. Plastic flowers sat permanently in the windows while fake grass sprouted at the base. The castle shouldn't have been anything to be scared of and yet for some reason he was filled with a sense of dread. Despite this, unable to stop himself, he took a step towards the playhouse. Then he noticed the legs. Stretching out of the front door of the castle was a pair of legs. They were long – long enough to belong to an adult man. The legs wore dirty black trousers and a pair of heavy-looking black boots on the feet.

'When the wind blows the cradle will rock …'

As he stepped even closer, Arthur realised it was a man's voice he was hearing. Only the man was singing in a false high-pitched tone. There was a window in the side of the castle closest to Arthur, but he couldn't see through it yet. He took another tentative step forward.

'When the bough breaks the cradle will fall …'

Arthur's breaths came raggedly as he stooped to look through the window at the man inside the playhouse.

'And down will come baby, cradle and all.'

He was dressed head to toe in black, a dirty long coat to match his trousers. His hair was long – falling well below his shoulders – greasy and blond with dark streaks of dirt matted into it. His beard was thick and bristly but patchy in places. What Arthur could see of his skin looked red and blotchy. He was singing to a baby doll cradled in his arms, but when Arthur peeked in, the man slowly turned his head and looked up at him. His thick eyebrows created a dark hood over his eyes, eyes that were terrifyingly familiar. He grinned from ear to ear, a grin Arthur recognised from his dreams.

The grin opened, revealing blackened and crooked teeth, and the man spoke in a dry, rasping voice. 'Hello, Arthur.'

CHAPTER THIRTEEN

As soon as the man in the playhouse spoke, Arthur turned and ran. One of his shoelaces had come loose and he tripped over it. He landed chin first on the floor, only just avoiding biting his tongue. Behind him, the man was standing up inside the playhouse, lifting it straight off the ground and giggling manically as he did. That was all the motivation Arthur needed. Ignoring the pain in his chin, he scrambled to his feet and fled. Legging it back down the escalators, he could hear the man laughing: a high-pitched cackle. Arthur went down the first escalator two steps at a time. He almost toppled over a second time and had to steady himself by gripping the moving handrail.

He was relieved to see shoppers and staff in the girls' section but still didn't feel safe enough to stop. He turned around and raced down the next escalator, bumping straight into Ash at the bottom.

'Whoa! Slow down, Arthur. What's the matter?' She'd paid for the train tracks and was holding them in a paper bag.

Arthur didn't slow down. He grabbed Ash's free hand and towed her out the front door in one hurried movement. He would have kept on running down the street if Ash hadn't ground to a halt, pulling him up with her.

'Arthur, wait! Will you please tell me what's wrong?'

He looked back in the direction of the toyshop. People shopping or out for a Sunday stroll walked along the street – all of them totally carefree. There was no sign of the man he'd seen in the playhouse.

'What is it, Arthur?'

He leaned against a shop window, catching his breath.

'I …' he began, 'I think I just saw Loki.'

'What? How?'

'No, that's wrong. I don't think I saw him. I know I saw him. It was definitely Loki. I can feel it. It was the same face I saw in my first dream but different. It's all scarred and old now.'

Ash looked as frightened as Arthur felt. 'What did he do?'

'He … He said my name.'

On the bus ride home, Arthur told Ash everything that had happened – the playhouse, the lullaby, what Loki had looked and sounded like.

'We have to tell someone,' she said.

'Who? Apart from Will, who'd believe us?'

'You're right. We're all alone in this.' She looked out the window and didn't speak again the rest of the way home.

The next morning, Arthur and Ash rushed to the bus stop as quickly as they could, not waiting for

Max and Stace. They wanted to fill Will in on the Loki encounter – they hadn't been able to tell him the previous evening as they still hadn't replaced the phones they'd lost in the river and Ash didn't know his landline number. In fact, they had been incapable of doing much the previous evening at all. When they'd gotten home, they'd packed the train tracks and train in a box for the presentation. Then they talked in circles, always coming to the same conclusion – that they shouldn't do anything until they knew more and that no one else would believe them. Eventually they went to their respective beds and tried to sleep. Arthur didn't drop off until after four in the morning and then only restlessly, tossing and turning and dreaming of the playhouse all through the night.

'Oh hi, guys!' Will said when he saw them coming to the bus shelter. 'Is that your presentation? I completely forgot to do any work on mine. I hope Rob didn't forget. Jeez.'

'Will, we need to tell you something,' Arthur said just as the bus pulled up. 'In fact, we need to tell you a lot.'

Judging by his friends' sober expressions, Will knew it was something very serious. 'What is it?'

****

'So you're saying that the Viking trickster god is somehow alive and well right here in Dublin and that he's probably trying to awaken this Jormungand thing, an ancient, giant snake that will destroy the world? And this snake is also buried under the city?'

'When you say it like that, it makes us sound crazy,' said Arthur.

'But is that what you're saying?' Will asked.

Arthur and Ash nodded their heads.

'I don't know what frightens me more,' said Will, 'the idea that it's true or the fact that I believe it.'

'You do?' Ash said.

'Yeah. Every word.' He paused for a moment then exclaimed, 'Something else just occurred to me! What if Loki was buried in a cave near the Jormungand?'

'And the drilling for the Metro somehow freed him,' Arthur added.

'Exactly.'

'But why Dublin?' asked Ash.

'Because it was the edge of the world,' Arthur replied. He had just worked it out. 'Ireland was the edge of the world as far as the Vikings were concerned. The edge of their world, anyway.' The bus was approaching the stop close to the school. 'Look, we have a lot more to talk about. Let's meet this evening. Dad works late these days so we can all meet in mine. We can say it's a sleepover. We'll get a DVD, popcorn, whatever.'

'Good idea,' Will said.

'How about eight o'clock?'

'Perfect,' said Ash, 'that'll give me time for a nap after school. I didn't sleep well last night.'

'Neither did I,' Arthur said grimly as the bus pulled up to the stop outside the school. 'Any time I was close, I just kept seeing his face. And hearing that laugh.'

※※※※※

The class presentations got off to a flying start. Ciara O'Connor and Brian Savage talked about the history of public transport in Dublin – which sounded boring to begin with, but they'd drawn their own comic strip to go with it. They handed a copy to everyone in the class. It showed cartoon versions of themselves travelling through time trying out the different modes of transport, from boats on canals to high-speed trains shuttling through underground tunnels. The O'Toole twins, Kevin and Colin, had found an old grainy video clip online that they played to the class. It showed men digging trenches for what would become the DART rail system in the 1970s. Megan Gallagher and Tara Egan acted out a scene of two passengers boarding the Metro for the first time, while Niall Fitzgerald and Mark Curtis – both wannabe rock stars – performed a song on the same topic to much applause and wolf whistles.

'Very good,' Miss Keegan said, clapping along with the class as the boys made their way back to their seats. 'Next we have Will and Rob.'

Will shrugged hopefully at Arthur and Ash as he walked up to the front of the class. Rob was carrying a cardboard box and laptop with him, which he set up on Miss Keegan's desk.

'Dynamite!' announced Rob theatrically. He took a red stick of dynamite out of the box. Or rather, a kitchen-paper tube painted to look like a stick of dynamite with a piece of wire sticking out of the top as the fuse. He showed it off to the class then handed it to Will. Will got the picture. He took the box and walked through the class, giving everyone their own cardboard stick of dynamite to take home. Arthur idly wondered where Rob had managed to find so many kitchen-paper tubes over the weekend.

Rob continued his presentation, talking about how dynamite had been used for excavating tunnels for over a hundred years and how it had been invented by accident by Alfred Nobel (whom the Nobel Prize was named after). He explained that, while modern drilling machinery like the massive EarthKruncher 5000 at Usher's Quay had made excavating a lot easier and more accurate, dynamite was still a necessary part of the process.

'Sometimes,' he said in conclusion, 'you just have to blow stuff up.' He pressed a key on the laptop and turned the screen towards the class. Video after video of explosions played on the screen to classical music. Some were demolitions; some were excavations; some were just random test explosions. When the video finished, the class gave them a round of applause. Arthur had to admit that Rob had done a good job; Will had been lucky.

'Thank you, Rob and Will,' Miss Keegan said, 'for a very interesting take on the presentation. Right, next up are Arthur and Ashling. I believe if everyone turns their seats around they'll be able to see better.'

Arthur and Ash had already set up their train tracks on a desk at the back of the class. When the other pupils were facing them, Ash flicked the switch to power the train. She operated the electronics as Arthur spoke about every stop on the line – all information he'd learned from Citi-Trak's website. Although he really had to struggle to keep in the yawns following his restless night, he thought he was doing surprisingly well. And the train itself ran smoothly over all the new track. When the Metro reached the end of the line, Arthur and Ash bowed to applause.

Just then, the school bell rang.

'Well, look at that!' said Miss Keegan. 'Time flies when you're having fun. Lunch already! Be back promptly in an hour. And by promptly, I mean right on time!'

The other presentations continued after lunch and Arthur was pleased to find that they took his mind off the terrifying encounter the previous day. On the bus ride home, however, his thoughts soon returned to it and it was clear from their expressions that Will and Ash were thinking about it too. Ash and Arthur parted from Will at the bus stop, reminding him to meet them in Arthur's house at eight o'clock that evening.

After dinner, Ash went up to her room. She hadn't been joking about trying to squeeze a nap in before the sleepover. She shut her curtains, as it was still bright out, and collapsed onto the bed. With a deep yawn, she closed her eyes and waited. An hour later, sleep still hadn't come. She'd been tossing and turning so much in an attempt to sleep that the sheets had become completely tangled underneath her. Golden late-afternoon sunlight streamed in through a gap in the curtains. She'd never been able to get to sleep if it was bright outside, even as a baby.

She gave in and sat up in the bed. She picked her laptop off the floor and opened the lid. It switched itself on automatically with a tinny electronic fanfare. Her desktop wallpaper showed a photograph of the first circuit board she'd ever made. It was only a basic FM radio but she still felt proud of it.

Ash opened up her web browser and redirected it straight to Google. She considered what to search for a moment, then typed in 'Jormungand'. She didn't think this would tell her anything more about the creature than they'd found out from Olaf, but it was worth a try. The screen was instantly full of images of the monster: old sketches, prints and paintings. In most of the pictures it was a giant snake battling armies of men. It flew above them, baring its fangs. In other pictures, it was depicted wrapped around a tree trunk as on Arthur's pendant.

She had another idea and typed in 'Viking pendants'. The search engine returned image after image of gold, silver and bronze pendants. Many featured the Jormungand design; many more featured faces. Some included the strange rune lettering they'd seen in the tunnel.

Her eyelids were finally starting to feel heavy as she looked at the page. She yawned, her head resting on her shoulder as she pressed the Page Down key. Without realising it, her lids began to gradually close. Her mind was flowing in and out of consciousness when suddenly something shocking flashed in her vision. She opened her eyes wide, thinking she'd dreamt it, but she hadn't. There it was, on the screen, clear as day! She pressed Print and leapt out of bed. She'd have to show Arthur straight away.

Arthur had just taken the popcorn out of the microwave when the doorbell rang. He took one look at the burnt popcorn, dropped it in the bin then answered the door. It was Ash.

'You're early,' he said.

'This was too important to wait,' she said and thrust a computer printout into his hand. 'Look what I found.'

He looked at the page then back to her.

'Is this …?'

'Yeah.'

'Can it be real?'

'I think so.'

He looked back down at the printout. It showed a silver Viking pendant. Like his own pendant, it was circular with a hole punched in the top for the necklace. A face was carved into this pendant, surrounded by runes similar to those they'd seen in the tunnel. Though the carving was made up of simple lines with cross-hatching for shading, there was no mistaking whose the face was – from the intelligent, watchful eyes, to the hair cropped short to the skull, to the cheeky grin. There was no doubt at all that the face on the pendant was Will's.

CHAPTER FOURTEEN

'How can this be?' Ash asked as Arthur stared at the printout. She looked over his shoulder at it, searching for any sign that she could have been mistaken.

'I don't know. But there's no doubt that it's Will.'

'So what does this mean?'

'I think it means he hasn't been telling us the whole truth,' Arthur said grimly.

'He'll be here soon. We'll just ask him.'

'There's no point in asking. If he'd wanted to tell us he'd have told us by now.'

'So what do you suggest?'

Arthur sat on the stairs. He felt the pendant in his pocket dig into his thigh. The weight of it reminded him of something. Something he'd thought odd at the time but had forgotten about till this instant. He took the pendant out and looked at it in the palm of his hand. It wasn't glowing now and hadn't done so since the last time he'd worn it.

'Ash, think back. Can you remember Will ever touching the pendant?'

She looked up to the ceiling, recalling every time they'd examined the pendant. 'No. In fact, I remember offering it to him and he wouldn't take it.'

'Thought so,' Arthur said. He stood back up. 'In that case, I have a plan.'

Moments later, Will arrived. Arthur greeted him with a smile and led him into the living room. Ash was already stretched out on the sofa, balancing a large bowl of fresh popcorn on her stomach and munching away. She was too engrossed in the soap opera on the TV to say 'hi' properly, so she just smiled with a full mouth.

'We were just watching this for a while,' Arthur said. 'We can have our talk when it's over.' He tapped Ash's legs and she sat up straight, making room for them both.

'No problem,' Will said as they sat either side of Ash.

Arthur reached into the bowl and took out a handful of popcorn, stuffing it into his mouth. Ash did the same and offered the bowl to Will. He chose one piece and popped it into his mouth.

'Take more,' she said, her mouth so full that some crumbs fell out. 'Arthur burned the first bag – clumsy – but I helped him make more. It's really good.'

'Okay, thanks.' Will laughed. 'Didn't they teach you how to make popcorn in Kerry?'

Arthur laughed too. Will reached in, took his own handful and tried to fit the whole fistful into his mouth.

Both Arthur and Ash giggled at him. They exchanged a quick glance, then looked back at the TV, pretending to watch the bad soap opera while really listening intently to the sound of Will munching the popcorn.

When his first fistful of popcorn was gone, he reached for more, diving his hand deep into the bowl. Suddenly there was a bright flash of green light, just like the one they'd experienced underwater a week ago.

Popcorn flew everywhere and Will leaped away from the bowl, as if in pain. He fell to the floor and held his hand to his chest, spluttering popcorn out of his mouth.

Arthur leapt up from the couch. 'I knew it!' he cried triumphantly as he took the bowl away from Ash. He picked out the pendant they'd hidden there moments before Will arrived and showed it to him.

Will's eyes widened in shock when he saw it. He kept rubbing his hand. It looked red, as if it had been scalded in hot water.

'I … I …' He struggled to find the words.

'Who and what are you?' demanded Ash, standing up next to Arthur.

'I … I …' he said again. 'Just … just don't jump to any rash conclusions. I can explain.'

'Well, you'd better start explaining fast,' Arthur said. He walked around the couch to stand directly over Will, holding out the pendant like it was a weapon.

'Okay.' Will scrambled to his feet and backed himself against a wall. 'Okay! Relax. Please, Arthur. I'll explain. Just sit down. I'm not going anywhere.'

Ash looked at Arthur, who was studying Will's face. Slowly he nodded and they both sat down on the popcorn-covered sofa. Will sat in the armchair opposite them.

'Where do I start?' Will said aloud to himself.

'With the truth,' Ash answered angrily.

'Okay. The truth. It's a long story.'

'We have time,' said Arthur.

'Do we, though?' Will took a deep breath and began. 'Everything you know about the Jormungand is true. The Vikings buried it in a cavern under Dublin, along with a hundred men to guard it until they died.'

'The men I saw in the vision I had in class,' Arthur exclaimed.

'Exactly. And from your dream the other night you figured out what must have happened to Loki. That he was captured by the other gods and sealed in a cave

186

under Dublin and that now he's escaped somehow. But you don't know the other lengths the Vikings went to to make sure the World Serpent couldn't escape.'

'Just get on with it, Will,' Ash demanded. 'Stop being so dramatic and tell us about the Jormungand and how you know all this.'

'Sorry. Well, the serpent had almost destroyed the world once and the gods didn't want it to happen again. So they charged a Viking family in Dublin, the Ó Dubhghaill family, with a sacred task: to protect not only the city but the world from another attack by the Jormungand. They were to make sure it never escaped. And if it did, they'd have to find a way to stop it. They were all trained warriors and the father was to pass the tradition on to his first-born son, and that son would pass it to his first-born son and so on down through the generations, so there would always be an Ó Dubhghaill in Dublin guarding the serpent.

'Eventually, after hundreds of years of protecting the world, the Ó Dubhghaill family name, like so many other names, changed and became the more

English-sounding "Doyle". From the moment I was old enough, my father told me all of this. He taught me what my responsibility to the world was. But he died before he could train me properly.'

Will stood up. He shook his hand and blew on it and the redness gradually subsided.

'He died before he could tell me how to stop the Jormungand.'

Arthur and Ash sat silently for a moment, letting all this sink in. Then Arthur pointed to Will's hand.

'But what about that?'

'The pendant has some kind of hidden powers that are unleashed when I touch it. Probably because I'm the last of the family. I only found that out when we almost drowned. I accidentally touched it trying to pull the grate off. The blast from it smashed the grate and freed us.'

'But it hurts you, doesn't it?' Arthur asked.

'Not really. It just feels strange. Like extra strong pins and needles running up your arm.'

'Is there anything else you haven't told us?' Ash asked.

'No, that's it,' said Will, sitting back down. 'That's the whole truth.'

Arthur and Ash considered Will sitting there, looking at his feet.

'I wanted to tell you sooner,' he added, 'but I didn't know how. It's a lot to take in.'

'Give us a minute, will you?' Arthur asked.

Will nodded, pushed himself out of the armchair and left the others alone in the living room.

'Well?' Ash started. 'What do you think?'

'I don't know what to think. He's right about one thing. It is a lot to take in. But I can't believe he didn't tell us this sooner, when he first realised what was going on.'

'I just wish he had. It would be easier to believe then. Now I'm not sure we can trust him.'

'True. But I guess I can see where he's coming from. Some things are hard to talk about.' He remembered how difficult it had been telling Ash and Will about his mother.

A full minute passed, the clock on the mantelpiece ticking away the seconds.

'In that dream I had,' Arthur said eventually, 'the Norns mentioned that a young boy and his friends could stop Loki.'

'So you think Will is that boy?'

'Well, it would make sense, wouldn't it?'

'I suppose. So what do we do now?'

He thought for a second before replying. 'We're going to need all the help we can get to stop this thing if it gets loose. I don't think we have any choice but to trust Will.'

Ash thought about it for a moment and then said, 'You're right, Arthur, I guess we should give him a second chance.'

They called Will back in. He took his place in the armchair again and looked at them anxiously.

'So?' he asked.

'I believe you,' Arthur said.

'So do I,' said Ash.

Will's face lit up. 'Thank you so much.'

'But no more secrets, agreed?' insisted Arthur.

'Agreed,' replied Will, clearly relieved they had accepted his explanation.

'So what now?' Ash asked.

'Now it's up to me as the last protector to stop this thing. I'll go back to the Poddle and I'll find the cavern and I'll figure out a way to prevent Loki from awakening the Jormungand.' He chuckled nervously. 'Easy peasy.'

'How will you do that?'

'Well, as dangerously obsessed with explosives as Rob Tynan is, he did make an interesting point. There's bound to be shed-loads of dynamite at the Metro site. I was thinking I might get some and use it to blow up the Jormungand. That's one weapon they didn't have a thousand years ago, and the only one I have a hope of getting hold of.'

'We'll help you,' Ash said, getting to her feet. Will's face lit up even more.

'Eh, no, we won't,' Arthur said from the couch.

'What?'

'We won't be helping,' Arthur said. 'In fact, Will, I don't think it's a good plan at all.'

'Why not?' Will asked.

'You want to steal a load of dynamite from my

191

dad's workplace, and go back to somewhere we almost drowned a few days ago to find a giant serpent and try to blow it up?' said Arthur, aghast. 'All the while there's an insane evil god chasing after you – and us! No, it's madness. It's way too dangerous. We could all be killed.'

'Well, what do you suggest?' Will asked. 'If we don't do something, the drilling could awaken the Jormungand and Loki will be able to free it to destroy the world.'

'I'll talk to my dad,' Arthur answered. 'I'll try to convince him to stop drilling. If they don't build the tunnel, the World Serpent won't wake up and Loki probably won't be able to find him.'

'And if that doesn't work?' Ash asked doubtfully.

'It has to,' he replied, with a touch of desperation in his voice, 'it just has to.'

CHAPTER FIFTEEN

The following morning, Ash and Will were still sound asleep on couch cushions on Arthur's bedroom floor when he got up to speak to Joe. He quietly threw back his covers and tiptoed over his sleeping friends. Following Will's revelations the previous night, they'd spent hours online, searching for more information about the Jormungand. They found nothing new – and definitely no clue as to how to stop it.

As usual, Joe was leaving early; the sun still hadn't risen fully in the sky. Arthur found him in the kitchen.

'Good morning, young man,' Joe said, surprised to see him. 'You're up early! How are your friends?'

'They're still asleep.'

Joe was packing sandwiches into a small cooler bag to take to work with him. Arthur hovered nearby, watching him. Joe zipped up the bag then turned to his waiting son.

'Something up, Arthur?'

'No. Not really.'

Joe took his car keys off the counter then Arthur added hurriedly, 'Well … kind of.'

Joe sat down at the kitchen table. He looked at his watch.

'Okay. I have a few minutes. Take a seat and tell me about it.'

Arthur sat opposite him. He didn't know how to start. What he was about to ask his father seemed so ridiculous in the almost-light of day. And he definitely couldn't be totally honest with Joe. Then he'd surely think Arthur had gone crazy.

'What if you found out it wasn't a good idea to build the tunnel?' he asked eventually.

'How do you mean?'

'Well, what if I asked you not to excavate it?'

'What's this about, Arthur? Is it because you want

to move back to Kerry?'

'No, it's not that. It's just … I don't think you should drill down there. I don't think anyone should. And you could stop it. You could say it's not safe and the whole thing would be cancelled. They'd find a different route or something.'

'I could. But it is safe. We know that, Arthur. There's nothing to worry about. We did geothermal scans of under the ground and nothing showed up.'

'Nothing that would show up anyway,' said Arthur.

'What are you talking about?'

'I can't explain it. But you have to trust me, Dad. Please get the project cancelled.'

Joe stood up, angry.

'Arthur, are you out of your mind? Ask them to stop a multi-million-euro job for no reason other than my son wants me to? That would be professional suicide!'

'Dad, just listen to me!'

'No, Arthur, I won't. This is ridiculous. I know this is just because you want to go back to Kerry and I don't want to hear another word about it. Now, I have to go or I'll be late for work.' He picked up his sandwiches and made for the front door, but the next words out of his son's mouth made him pause.

'Mum would have listened to me.'

Joe stopped for a second then turned on the spot. He suddenly looked very old, very tired, his skin drawn across his face with dark bags under his eyes. 'Well, she's not here, Arthur,' he said quietly. 'I'm afraid I'm all you have.' He turned and left the house in a hurry, both furious and disappointed. Arthur sat by himself in the kitchen with a lump in his throat. Eventually he made his way back upstairs and into bed.

※※※※※

On the way to school, Arthur lied to Will and Ash about having talked to Joe. He didn't have the heart to tell them how badly it had gone.

'I'll talk to him this evening,' he promised.

The rest of the day went very slowly. Miss Keegan had joked about Arthur, Will and Ash wanting to go for their weekly swim. Arthur was shocked it had only been a week since they'd almost drowned in the tunnel.

So much had happened in the meantime: his whole view of the world had been turned upside down.

The three of them avoided the subject of Loki and the Jormungand all day. Ash and Will sensed correctly that Arthur didn't want to talk about it.

'Let's not mention it till he's talked to his dad this evening,' Ash said to Will when she got a chance. He agreed and that was the way they left it.

During class, Miss Keegan twice noticed that Arthur was distracted and had to scold him. He half-heartedly apologised each time and went back to thinking about what his dad had said.

Finally, the school day ended. Will went home while Ash and Arthur both returned to Arthur's empty house. Although Ash had no reason to be there, she didn't want to leave Arthur on his own just yet. She just had a feeling that he needed the company.

The moon had risen by the time Joe finished work for the day. The darkness in the sky was even more pronounced at the Metro site, where the bright work lights contrasted with the blackness above and created sharp shadows here and there. Everyone else in the Citi-Trak office had gone home hours ago, but Joe had stayed back to finish some paperwork. Ruairí had offered to stay with him but Joe sent him home.

Joe signed his last blueprint for the day, dropped it in a paper folder and then into a filing cabinet. He slung his coat over his shoulder, picked up his keys and left the office, locking it behind him. The click of the lock sounded unnaturally loud in the silence of the site.

It was much colder outside than he'd thought it would be and he shivered when an icy breeze penetrated his clothing. He put on his coat, making sure to zip it right up to his neck, and rubbed his hands together vigorously.

Thunk!

He hadn't even time to wonder what the sound was before he heard it a second time.

Thunk!

It sounded like two pieces of heavy metal knocking together.

Thunk!

It came a third time and this time he was able to pinpoint the sound. It was coming from behind the office prefab, where the storage containers were. He hesitated for a minute but then figured that somebody might be in trouble. They might have been accidentally locked into one of the containers. It had happened on another site he'd worked on a couple of years ago. As dangerous as it had been, at least it was the height of the summer then. If somebody was locked into a container on this freezing night, they could end up catching pneumonia or worse. He considered calling the security man stationed at the gate but then decided to find out what the noise was before disturbing him – besides, there might be a simple explanation and he didn't want to look like a fool. Maybe a fox or some other animal had gotten trapped. He pulled up his coat collar against the cold and started walking towards the containers.

'Hello?' he called out. No answer. 'Anyone there?'

He heard another *thunk* followed briskly by a *thud*, as if something had dropped to the ground.

'Is someone back there?' he called again. Still no reply. He approached the storage area. Long shipping containers were stacked in three rows of five. They housed all the materials the crew needed for excavating: safety equipment, gear for welding, drilling, hosing and nailing, spray-paint cans, ladders, ropes, screws and glue to name just a few. All the containers in the first row seemed fine at first glance, as did the second row. But the door to the middle container in the last row was wide open. 'DANGER!' was painted in bold red letters on the front. He heard someone moving about inside.

'Who's in there?' As he walked towards the open container, his feet crunched on the gravel. The harsh work lights cast his shadow far against the side of the containers, making it look like Joe was a giant. When he got near the open door, he saw the padlock lying on the ground, split open. He reached the opening and looked inside.

At first it was difficult to see, but gradually his eyes became accustomed to the gloom. A tall, dark figure was hunched over, reading the labels on the wooden crates stacked inside. He was leaning on a shovel.

'Hey! Who are you?' Joe asked, hoping the nervousness he was feeling couldn't be heard in his voice. 'How did you get past security?'

The figure turned quickly, startled. He had long straggly hair and a matching beard. Even though the work lights were faint here, Joe could still make out his grin stretching from ear to ear.

'Oh …' said the man in a croaky rasp, 'Willie and I go way back.'

'What are you doing here?'

'I apologise. It's Hallowe'en soon so I was just playing trick or treat.' He patted one of the boxes, taking a step towards Joe. 'You have the treats …' He took another step forward. 'And I have the tricks.' With that he suddenly swung the shovel in his hand, whacking Joe in the ribs. He swung a second time and caught him across the shins.

'Argh!' Joe cried out in pain as he crumpled to the ground. He'd heard a loud crack when the man had hit him first and, from the agonising spasm shooting up his side, he could only assume that the blow had broken a couple of ribs.

'Oh dear me!' said the man in mock concern. 'Where are my manners?' He bent over Joe, leering down at him. 'Allow me to introduce myself. I'm a friend of your son's.' Joe heard the shovel slicing through the air once more and fell unconscious the instant it collided with the side of his head.

※※※※※

Arthur was surprised to find a garda standing outside when he answered the door. He was tall, with wavy ginger hair and pale green eyes. He was holding his hat to his chest. His squad car was parked in the drive, blue lights flashing. The old lady across the street with the dog had ventured out to take a look.

'Hello, son. Are you Arthur Quinn?' asked the garda.

'Yes.'

'Son of Joe Quinn?'

'Yeah, that's me.'

'I'm Garda Morrissey,' he said, showing him his identification. 'Can I come in? I need to speak to you.'

As Arthur led the garda into the living room, he imagined the worst. There'd been an accident at work with the drill. Or the Jormungand had somehow gotten out and – he didn't want to think about what would have happened if that was the case.

Ash looked up from the couch where she'd been watching TV.

'Is something wrong?' she asked, getting to her feet.

'I don't know,' Arthur answered.

The three of them sat down, the garda in the armchair that Will had sat in the night before.

'Is it about Dad?'

'Yes, Arthur,' said Garda Morrissey, 'it's your father. There's no easy way to say this. He was attacked at his workplace a couple of hours ago. Attacked badly. He's alive, but … well, he's not in a good condition. He's in the hospital and I'd like to take you to see him now.'

Tears were already running down Arthur's face when he got up. Though shocked and anxious for Joe, he was also relieved that at least he was still alive. Ash put her arm around him.

'If you're ready to come now, Arthur?'

'Can Ash come?' Arthur asked.

'I suppose so. Just call your parents first, Miss. We should leave now. The sooner, the better.'

※※※※※

Ruairí and Deirdre were in the waiting room when Garda Morrissey led Arthur and Ash into the hospital. They rushed to meet them.

'I'm so sorry,' Ruairí said.

'The security guard found him and called us,' added Deirdre. 'Brace yourselves. He's ... eh ... he's in a bad way.'

Arthur could only manage to nod. Ash thanked them. Garda Morrissey laid his hands on Arthur's shoulders.

'Do you feel up to this?' he asked.

Arthur nodded again. The garda led him into a private room.

Joe was unconscious in the hospital bed. He was topless, with a large gauze bandage wrapped tightly around his chest and ribs. More bandage was wrapped around his forehead. The whole left side of his face was swollen to the size of a large grapefruit and discoloured to a dark purple. Stitches ran across his cheek where he'd been cut. His right leg was in a cast and suspended above him by sturdy wires. A drip fed into his arm, while a heart monitor was clamped to his index finger. It beeped steadily on the screen next to the bed.

There was a nurse in the room checking the drip.

Arthur choked back a sob and said, 'Is he going to be all right?'

'His wounds are serious, but I'm sure with a bit of time and lots of rest he'll be grand,' said the nurse kindly, squeezing Arthur's shoulder as she left.

Arthur sat looking at his father for a long time. Joe's breathing was coming in ragged bursts; from the wheezing sound he made, it was clearly difficult for him. Garda Morrissey sat in the room with Arthur, looking out the window. Eventually, Arthur got to his feet. He took his father's limp hand.

'I'll get him,' he whispered. 'I'll get the thing who did this.' He stepped out into the hallway, leaving the garda to watch over his father. While Arthur had been in the room with Joe, Will had turned up and was sitting with Ash; Ruairí and Deirdre had left.

'I came as soon as I heard,' Will said. 'I'm so sorry, Arthur.'

Arthur looked at them both coldly.

'Tomorrow,' he said.

'Tomorrow?' repeated Ash.

'Tomorrow. We go back to the tunnel tomorrow night, destroy the serpent, stop Loki and end this once and for all.'

CHAPTER SIXTEEN

Garda Morrissey took Ash and Will home a little before midnight and then returned to sit with Arthur who had refused to leave. Arthur didn't sleep at all that night and he didn't go to school either the following day. He stayed sitting by Joe's hospital bed, watching his dad's uneven and laboured breathing. At one stage, he rubbed his cheeks. Joe hadn't shaved for a couple of days and the stubble appearing on his face was coarse and itchy. He might never get to shave himself again. As soon as the thought had formed in Arthur's mind, he regretted it.

The garda had gone off duty at five o'clock in the morning. He'd offered again to take Arthur home, but

Arthur had once more refused, settling himself deep into the hard armchair by the bed. Some time after lunch on the Wednesday, Arthur nodded off to sleep.

✳✳✳✳✳

In a time before written history, in Asgard, the realm of the gods, Odin's great steed gallops across the land, scooping large clumps of earth from the ground. The other gods and goddesses follow him in their chariots, barely keeping pace. The sky is dark overhead with black clouds threatening thunderstorms. There will be no thunder today, though. Thor, the thunder god, is gone to battle with the Jormungand. But it is not the serpent that concerns the gods. It is Loki. He rides in a chariot alongside his human wife. She has been warned not to speak to him and to ignore any movement from him. His arms and legs are tied together like a hog's and his mouth is gagged. The Norns promised there was a cavern at the edge of the world that could hold him and that is where the gods are going on this heavy day.

They come to the top of a rainbow which curves

downwards and away from them, over the edge of a sheer cliff. The rainbow is known as Bifrost and it is the bridge from Asgard, land of the gods, to anywhere in Midgard, land of man. Odin stops at the edge of Asgard and turns to his gods.

'We ride for Dubh Linn!' he announces then kicks his steed forward onto the great rainbow bridge.

The others follow, Loki's chariot first, where they can all keep an eye on it. Bifrost is wide and strong enough to carry them all. It doesn't so much as shudder under the weight of the gods, their chariots and their animals. They ride downwards on the sloping bridge, through the sky and away from Asgard. Green land rises before them. They can see a pair of rivers and a human settlement: stone and mud huts for houses and a high stone wall around the perimeter. This is Dubh Linn, the city at the edge of the world. In the future, it will be known as Dublin.

Odin arrives first, his steed bounding off Bifrost and onto the frost-covered land of the Irish town. The All Father waits on his horse until all the chariots have disembarked from the bridge.

'There!' he says to them, pointing in the direction of one of the rivers. Next to the riverbed is a large hole in the ground. It gapes wide and deep, as if a mouth had opened in the earth itself: the entrance to the cavern the Norns promised. Odin leads the way in and down through the cave. Jagged rocks surround the opening, making it seem more like a mouth with fangs than the gods are happy to think about.

From the opening, rock and earth slope downward on a gradual incline that is gentle enough for the animals and chariots to make their way down. Loki's eyes bulge at the sight of the dark cave around him. His wife continues to ignore him. She knows he has done wrong and now it's time to pay, and she has chosen to stay with him, whatever the cost. Water drips somewhere in the distance, echoing throughout the cavern, and stalactites hang low over their heads. As Odin rides down, he rubs his hand along the rock face. The walls are damp. It is cold, dark and empty: a suitable place for Loki's punishment for what he has unleashed on the world.

They come to the open cavern. Although 'open'

is not the best word to describe it. It's true that it has a high ceiling with one massive stalactite in the centre, but the surrounding walls are close and the atmosphere claustrophobic. A stone table sits in the middle, directly below the huge stalactite.

Odin dismounts from his horse and looks up at the stalactite with his one good eye. Then he looks at the altar underneath. A suitable place indeed.

'Bring forth the Father of Lies,' he calls to the other gods. Vidar and Vali, youngest sons of Odin, lift Loki from his chariot and carry him to the altar. They lay him on top as his human wife steps around next to them; then they bind him to the altar itself.

'Ungag him,' Odin says. Some of the gods start to protest but Odin speaks over them. 'He deserves one last chance to redeem himself. Ungag him.'

The two gods untie the gag from around Loki's mouth. He sighs and stretches his jaws with a loud click.

'Ah now!' Loki says. 'That's much more comfortable. Although I could do without the bindings around my arms and legs.' He smiles wryly.

'You'll have to get used to them, Loki,' says Odin.

'That's a shame.'

'Listen to me well, Loki,' Odin says. 'You are the Father of Lies, the Lie-smith, the Trickster God. You are my half brother. What you have unleashed on the world is truly terrible. The Jormungand and your other brood bring nothing but sadness and pain. Their only motive is to spill tears and blood. Because of your beasts, families have been left fatherless, whole towns and villages have ceased to exist, the world as we have known it could be torn asunder.'

The All Father takes a step forward and rests a hand on Loki's shoulder.

'Now is your chance, half-brother Loki. Redeem yourself and this punishment need not take place.'

Loki looks up at Odin through teary eyes. 'Redemption? You're offering me redemption?'

Odin simply nods. The other gods wait in silence while Loki's human wife merely hopes.

Suddenly Loki spits at the All Father. A great wad of phlegm stains his brown woollen tunic.

'That's what I think of your redemption!' Loki screams, laughing.

Odin looks down at the stain then back to Loki.

'So it goes. You had your chance,' he mutters. He strides back to his horse and plunges his hand deep into the saddlebag. When he has found what he's looking for, he returns to the altar. In one hand he holds a bowl; in the other he holds a writhing venomous snake. The bowl is small and shallow. It is made of plain and undecorated red clay. He hands it to Loki's human wife.

'If you truly wish to help Loki,' he says to her, 'you will need this.'

Then he holds the snake towards Loki. It's a viper, tongue lashing out and fangs exposed. It keeps lunging for Loki's face but Odin has it tightly wrapped around his wrist.

'This will be your tormentor,' he says, 'as you have tormented the world with your own World Serpent. I have granted this snake the gift of agelessness. From this day forth, it will never age nor sicken. It will guard you for eternity.'

Loki raises a quizzical eyebrow at Odin but the All Father just looks at the human wife once more.

'I take away your appetites, woman. For food and water and air. You, however, will not be granted agelessness – despite your loyalty to your husband you do not deserve to share his eternal punishment. Now, have that bowl ready,' he says. Then he flings the snake towards the rock ceiling. Rather than fall back down to earth, the snake coils itself around the large stalactite. It looks down at Loki, fangs bared. Then a single bead of bright green venom forms at the tip of one of the fangs. It hangs there for a second before falling off. The venom drops through the cavern and lands right on Loki's forehead. He yells out in pain but doesn't have time to recover before another pearl of venom falls from the mouth of the snake onto his face. As he cries out again, his human wife now sees the importance of the bowl. She holds it over Loki's face, catching the next drop that falls.

'That will be your punishment,' Odin states. 'The venom will fall for all eternity, dulling your mind. The only relief will be your wife catching the drops. However, when the bowl is full, she will have to go and empty it. During these moments, you will suffer true excruciating pain. Each drop represents a life you took with your children.'

'You think this will stop me?' Loki cries, the pain starting to subside. 'I'll be back. And when I am, I'll start Ragnarok. The end of everything. The end of man, the end of gods. The end of all of you.'

The gods cannot hear him. They have left already, sealing the cave behind them. As Loki rants, the bowl his human wife is holding fills up. She walks off deep into the cavern to empty it. More venom falls onto his face and the ground shakes with his roars of pain. *Drip-drip-drip*.

❋❋❋❋❋

Someone was shaking Arthur's shoulder. He opened his eyes and looked up groggily. Garda Morrissey was back and standing over him.

'You fell asleep in the chair,' he said.

'Sorry. What time is it?'

'Just after six. Time to go home, son. You need proper rest too.'

Arthur rubbed the sleep out of his eyes and nodded blearily to the garda. He looked at his dad, still unconscious in the bed. The bruising under his eye had darkened and an ugly yellow discolouration had spread to the rest of his face. His breathing was just as strained as it had been the night before.

Arthur took Joe's free hand and whispered, 'I'll be back before you know it.'

'Don't worry, son,' Garda Morrissey said. 'He'll be awake in no time.'

'I hope so.'

The dream was still fresh in his mind on the drive home. So now he knew what had happened to Loki. He considered the new evidence that the dream had given him and guessed that the cave-in a few weeks ago had somehow killed the snake, allowing Loki's mind to clear and letting him plan his escape. While he thought, he barely heard Garda Morrissey speaking.

'Your friend, Ashling, is that her name?' he was saying from the driver's seat. 'Anyway, her parents called up the station this morning. They said they'd take you in since your extended family all live in

Kerry. Just until your father gets better. If that's all right with you?'

'That's perfect,' Arthur said, looking out the window. People were wrapped up tightly against the brisk wind and a light drizzle fell from the dark clouds. The sky reminded Arthur of the day the gods left Asgard.

Will was also in Ash's house when Garda Morrissey dropped Arthur off. They'd used the cover story of another sleepover and they both nodded at him grimly when he entered. How Ash's parents didn't realise they were up to something, Arthur would never know. They all ate dinner in silence, interrupted only by Max's non-stop chattering.

'How about some dessert?' Ash's mum said, clearing away their dishes. 'Some ice-cream?'

'No thanks,' Arthur said.

'Really? It's Triple Choc Swirl.'

'No, it's all right, Mom,' said Ash, 'we have homework to do.'

'That's a first,' joked her dad as the three of them bounded up the stairs to Ash's bedroom.

'How's your dad?' she asked Arthur, shutting the door behind her.

'The same,' he replied. He sat down on her bed next to Will.

'And are you sure it was Loki?' she said.

'Of course it was Loki!' Will said. 'Who else could it have been?'

'He's right,' Arthur said. 'It can't be a coincidence. What about you two? Any luck with what we talked about?'

Will and Ash looked at each other.

'A little bit,' Ash said. 'Are you sure you want to go through with this tonight?'

'Of course I am.'

'Well it's just … it's so soon after your dad –'

'I've never been more ready for anything, Ash.'

'Okay. Well I found this.' She handed him a computer printout from her desk.

Arthur looked at the confusing graph. It looked like a map or blueprint but he didn't know what of. He raised his eyebrows quizzically at her.

'It's a map,' she explained, 'of the Metro site. Do

you see those red squares? They're storage containers; it's where they keep all their equipment. And that container I've marked with the "X" is the one with the dynamite.'

'Wow,' he said, impressed. 'This is great. Where'd you find it?'

She blushed slightly. 'I hacked into the Citi-Trak website and got access to their internal server. It was all pretty easy. I also made us these ...'

She threw a torch into his lap. The seams had been sealed tightly with duct tape.

'Waterproof flashlights,' she explained, 'just in case.'

'These are great,' Arthur said, admiring her work, 'but hopefully, if we time it right, we won't need the waterproofing.'

'That shouldn't be a problem,' said Will. 'We'll have about three and a half hours. I checked in the school library. I remembered they have this book that I saw before, called the *Almanac* or something. It predicts the weather for every day of the year, stuff like that. And it also tells you the times of the tides.

The tide will be at its lowest in the Poddle at 4.05 in the morning and it'll start flooding in again at 7.23.'

'That should be lots of time,' Arthur agreed.

'So we were thinking,' Ash said, 'if we sneak out at two in the morning, it'll take about an hour to get to Usher's Quay, giving us another hour or so to break in and "borrow" the dynamite.' She preferred to say 'borrow' rather than 'steal', even though she didn't imagine they'd be bringing it back.

'Sounds good to me. We should get some sleep soon then.'

As they continued to work out the finer points of their plan, none of them heard the creak outside Ash's bedroom door. And none of them noticed Max, his ear pressed to the keyhole, listening to every word they were saying. And coming up with his own plan.

CHAPTER SEVENTEEN

Beep-beep-be–

Ash switched off her alarm clock midway through the third ring. She turned on the bedside lamp and rolled out of bed, already fully dressed. Arthur and Will were climbing out of sleeping bags on her floor, both also in warm clothing and both rubbing sleep from their eyes. No one spoke as they readied themselves and left the house, taking each step carefully to avoid creaking.

The night sky was cloudless – no doubt part of the reason that it was so cold – and the moon hovered brightly above the city. They went around to the side of the house where Ash had hidden two bicycles earlier in the evening; Arthur was going to ride Stace's bike, which she rarely used any more, with Will sitting on the crossbar. This arrangement worked out well since Will had never learned to cycle. He was carrying a backpack on his shoulders as they got onto the bikes.

'What's in there?' whispered Arthur, tapping the bag.

'School uniforms and stuff. I figured we'd have to go straight from the tunnel.'

'School really wasn't on my list of priorities. But good thinking all the same,' Ash said in a low voice as they rode off.

Cycling through the quiet city at 2 a.m. on a Wednesday morning was an experience Arthur wouldn't soon forget. The route they'd mapped out took them down side streets and back alleys. They chose this rather than the busier main roads to avoid being spotted by any curious gardaí. All was silent and still. The only thing Arthur saw moving the whole way to Usher's Quay was a fox scavenging in some bins. As the bikes approached, the fox looked up, its eyes shining green under the streetlights, and ran off into some nearby bushes.

A high wall, constructed from chipboard and painted with a repeating pattern of the Citi-Trak logo, ran around the entire perimeter of the Metro site. They skidded their bikes to a stop along the gravelly, unfinished path and surveyed the wall.

'How will we get over?' Ash wondered out loud.

Will got off the crossbar and pointed to a rubbish bin by the side of the road. 'We can stand on that and pull ourselves up. We should be able to make it.'

Just then, a third bike skidded around the corner next to them.

'Hi guys!' said Max, bounding off the bicycle happily.

Ash let her own bike crash to the ground. She grabbed him and shook him by the shoulders. 'What are you doing here? Did you follow us?'

Arthur pulled her away, allowing Max to explain himself.

'I heard you talking about going out. So I just hid in the hallway and followed you here. I almost lost you. You're a fast cycler, Arthur.'

'Max,' said Ash, kneeling down to get eye-to-eye with him, 'this is dangerous. Really dangerous. You have to go home.'

'He can't go home on his own, Ash,' Arthur reasoned.

Will laid his hand on her shoulder. 'He can come in with us. We'll take care of him. It's safer than making him wait out here or going home alone.'

'Really?' she sneered sarcastically. 'Is it really safer?' She took a deep breath, considering the options and quickly realised that, although she hated to admit it, Will was right in a way. It would be very unsafe for Max to cycle all the way home on his own at this time of night in what could be a dangerous city – if something happened to him there would be no one around to help him. And they couldn't leave him on the site: the security guard might find him and that would blow all their plans. Reluctantly she realised they had no other option than to take him along. 'All right. I guess we don't really have a choice. Max, stay close to me at all times. And don't touch anything.'

'I won't,' he promised.

She looked him straight in the eye again. 'And if something happens, just get out of the tunnel and run straight to the security guard on the site. Okay? Get help.'

'I will,' he said, starting to look a bit scared. 'Don't worry.'

They locked their bikes and clambered onto the bin one by one. Will went first, balancing precariously on the top of the wall to help Max over. They were quickly followed by Ash, then Arthur was the last to vault over the wall. He landed heavily on some dried mud. Ash was already consulting the map, working out the best way to reach the storage containers without being caught by security.

The work lights mounted on thirty-foot poles throughout the site cast their shadows deep and dark as they scuttled towards the storage area. Finding their way around the site had been easier than they'd thought and locating the storage units was even simpler than the confusing map had hinted. On their way they passed the prefab office they'd been in on their school tour. The lights were on inside. Arthur waved to the others to duck down. He put his finger to his lips then walked sideways like a crab, inching his way along the outside wall of the office. His fingers gripped the edge of the windowsill and he cautiously pulled himself up then peered into the office. The young engineer, Ruairí, was inside. He was keeled over at one of the desks, fast asleep. His head rested on a pile of plans and blueprints and drool from his mouth slowly dripped onto the paper. He held a half-eaten fried chicken leg in his left hand while his right arm was wrapped around a cardboard bucket of chicken pieces.

Arthur turned back to his friends. 'It's okay,' he whispered, 'he's fast asleep.' They crept past the prefab and on towards the storage area.

'This is it,' said Ash, as they came across the rows of containers. The one marked on the map with the dynamite was the centre container in the third row. Arthur shone his flashlight on the shut door. The word 'DANGER!' was painted there. It was like a warning for the rest of the night.

'Great,' he muttered sarcastically when he saw the

thick padlock that was keeping the door shut.

'No problem,' said Will, pulling a long instrument from his backpack. It consisted of a pair of steel blades at the end of two long arms. Joe owned a tool just like it: a bolt-cutter. Will positioned the blades over the lock then the four of them pushed the arms together. It took quite a bit of effort but they managed to snap through the lock.

The entrance swung open with a loud, rusty screech. Arthur's torch wasn't strong enough to light up the inside properly, so Will switched on his flashlight as well, illuminating the interior of the container. Wooden crates were stacked neatly against the back wall. 'WARNING!' was painted across each box in bold red letters, 'EXPLOSIVES'.

'Guess we're in the right place,' Arthur said, taking a large canvas shopping bag out of his backpack. They started filling the bag with the bright red sticks of the explosive.

'Who's there?' someone called from outside. 'Is someone in there?' It was Ruairí. The screeching of the container door must have woken him. It sounded like he was still a little way off and was probably just outside the office prefab. Arthur looked at Ash, Max looked at Will, then they all looked at each other. None of them so much as took a breath.

'Hello? I heard something. Who's there?'

Arthur frantically pointed at the bag of explosives and then to the door. He kept his finger to his lips so they'd know to be quiet. He picked up a handle of the bag but it was so heavy that he could barely budge it. Will took the second handle and, between them, they carried it out into the night air, their feet treading as lightly on the gravel as they could. They could hear Ruairí's approaching footsteps.

As Arthur and Will carried the bag in the opposite direction to the footsteps, Ash and Max carefully pushed the container door shut. They all winced as it creaked slightly, and Arthur turned and waved for them to leave the door and just follow him.

All four of them managed to tiptoe around the side of the last container just as Ruairí entered the row.

'What's this then?' he murmured to himself when he saw the half-open container. 'Is somebody there?'

They pushed themselves against a container wall, each too afraid to even blink. As Ruairí slowly approached the open door, his footsteps grew louder. In the tense silence Arthur could hear his heart pounding loudly in his ears.

When Ruairí got to the container, he eased the door open and peered carefully inside, ready to jump back quickly if anyone took a swing at him. Upon finding it empty save for the wooden crates, he pushed the door all the way shut. It made a slamming sound that echoed all over the site.

'Huh,' he said to himself, 'must have just been the wind.' Someone should really make sure these things are closed and locked properly, he thought. Looking around one final time but seeing nothing out of the ordinary, he proceeded to walk back to the office – and his bucket of fried chicken. Arthur counted a full two minutes in his head before he turned to the others and nodded. As silently as they could, they all lifted the bag and started to retrace their steps. As they returned through the corridor of containers, they slunk further into the shadows. When they passed the office, they weren't surprised to find Ruairí asleep once more. They hurried on.

'Do you think we have enough?' asked Ash, looking into the bag between them.

'I guess we'll know when we get down there,' answered Will.

'Get down where?' asked Max as they walked towards the dark opening to the Metro tunnel.

The drill lay dormant in the tunnel when they got there. Max ran to it for a closer look but Ash briskly called him back, reminding him of his promise to stay close. They rested the bag of dynamite beside the grate to the Poddle. Will prised it open. Straight away, they could smell the familiar stench and feel the cold air rising. Shivers ran up Arthur's spine at the memory of his last visit to the river. Ash leaned in for a closer look. Her hand rubbed against his. He looked up at her, surprised. She blushed then went to move back but he took her hand and squeezed it once. She smiled in gratitude and Arthur let her go.

'Scared, Max?' Will asked, stepping back from the hole in the ground.

'No,' replied Max, his eyes wide and fearful. He was beginning to regret his decision to join his sister and the two older boys on their night-time adventure. 'I'm not scared of anything.'

Will took a rope out of his backpack and handed it to Arthur. He then climbed down the ladder first, as Arthur and Ash tied one end of the rope to the bag with the dynamite.

'Ready!' Will shouted up. The others twisted the rope around their arms and slowly lowered the bag of explosives down the shaft. Even Max took up the slack at the end and gave a hand.

'Slowly, slowly!' Will yelled up again. 'Okay, I have it!' He guided the bag onto the damp stone floor then looked back up. 'Come on down.'

They climbed down, first Arthur, then Max and lastly Ash, Will shining his flashlight up the shaft to make it easier for them to see the rungs of the ladder. Max didn't complain once on the way down and

Arthur and Ash were relieved that he seemed to be taking it all in his stride. Arthur assumed that he was just happy to be spending time with them and made a mental note to play with Max more after this was all over – that was if they all made it out. He quickly pushed that thought away.

They all switched on their torches. The improved lighting didn't show up much of interest apart from a clearer view of the brick walls. The water was just above ankle height and already soaking into their socks. Arthur checked the time – it was 3.52, which gave them over three hours to get out before the place flooded. They started walking down the tunnel, now familiar with the slippery terrain. Arthur and Will carried the heavy bag between them.

'Don't let it get in the water,' Arthur warned. 'I remember Dad saying that it made dynamite useless.'

Before they knew it, they'd reached the fork in the tunnel. Again, they took the stone tunnel leading to the right. With the flashlights, Arthur could make out the strange carvings on the wall. The pendant was, as always, in his pocket and, even without its power hanging around his neck, he knew what the runes said. He'd written it himself in class thanks to the pendant: 'BEWARE THE JORMUNGAND'. It really was just like the 'WARNING' sign on the explosives container.

'Wow,' Max said, noticing the runes. 'This place is kind of creepy.'

'Are you okay?' asked Ash. He nodded with a smile but still reached for her hand. She held it tight. 'I've been wondering, why did the Vikings divert this part of the Poddle underground?' said Ash.

'It was the only way they'd be able to transport the Jormungand,' Will explained. 'It's massive, remember, and very heavy. Easier to move on rafts. And then, I guess, when the engineers made the rest of the tunnel during the last century they just left the Viking part as it was.'

'That would explain why the other part of the tunnel seems newer,' Arthur said.

They continued further than they had the last time, although Arthur had travelled this far in his vision. He recognised the carvings on the wall and looked ahead for the turn to the right that he knew should be coming up. His heart pounded faster as he thought of the men who'd travelled down here a thousand years ago to keep the Jormungand imprisoned.

'It's just around the corner,' he said.

'What is?' asked Ash.

'Wherever the Jormungand is. I saw it in that vision in class.'

They cautiously turned the corner and came face to face with –

'A dead end!' Ash exclaimed.

They rushed forward to the stone wall ahead of them. It was indeed a dead end: a completely solid rock surface with the same runes carved deep across it. But aside from those and a small groove in the centre, the wall was smooth and seamless. A drain to the left made a soft trickling sound as the the water from the Poddle escaped.

'We came all the way here for nothing?' cried Ash in dismay.

'No,' Arthur said, 'it can't be. In the vision, they went down the tunnel, turned the corner and went through here.'

'Arthur, look,' said Will, pointing at his jeans' pocket. When Arthur looked down, he was shocked to see it was glowing green. Or, rather, the pendant inside was glowing green. He took it out. It was glowing brighter and more vividly than it ever had before. He studied the dead end again. He put the pendant up to the letters and it glowed brighter still. Then he moved it closer to the groove in the wall. The green light pulsed off it rapidly.

He pushed the pendant into the groove – it was a perfect fit. He counted in his head to ten but nothing happened, so he tried turning it left and then right, but still nothing happened, so finally he pulled the pendant out and dropped it back into his pocket, dejected.

'Guess we'll have to try something el–'

Suddenly, there was a low rumbling sound and the ground started to vibrate. Slowly the wall started to slide to one side. It opened like an elevator door, exposing a wide cavern behind it. As in Arthur's vision, the cavern was lit by a hundred flickering torches mounted on the stone walls. An iron shield hung beneath each torch.

They were a variety of colours and patterns, some with snakes on them, others showing wolves, while some even depicted monstrous-looking women.

'There it is,' said Will, striding into the cavern. They all followed in awe, jaws hanging open.

The Jormungand looked like it was nearly a hundred feet long, and it was lying curled in the centre of the cavern. Standing near it, they could guess that its body had at least a seven-foot diameter and that it was wide enough to swallow a grown man whole and on his side. Each scale on its expansive body was twice the size of Arthur's hand; they were shiny, too, and appeared to glitter in a variety of reds and greens. Although the Jormungand was known as the World Serpent, it was much more than just a snake. A massive ribbed and leathery wing lay still on each side of its body, while four small legs with feet ending in vicious-looking claws were attached to its belly. The legs were tiny compared to the rest of the beast and reminded Arthur of pictures he'd seen of Tyrannosaurus Rex. Three ridged fins ran over the beast's head and its eyes and mouth were closed. It looked so peaceful that Arthur wondered if it was alive at all. But then he noticed slits on the side of its head opening and closing, just like gills, as the serpent breathed in and out.

'Just like the legend said,' Ash commented. 'Asleep for an eternity.'

'Look at that!' exclaimed Arthur. Beyond the Jormungand was a Viking ship. With no water in the cavern, it was tilted slightly to one side. It looked just like the pictures of Viking longboats he'd seen in films and history books. It had low sides, with spaces for oars for rowing, and the bow curved dramatically upwards. At the top of the bow was the carved wooden head of a dragon. The stern also swept upwards and ended in a carved swirl. A red and white striped sail hung limply from the mast with no wind to fill it.

'How did they get that in here?'

'They must have built it in here,' Arthur explained. 'I remember seeing some of the men with building materials and tools in my vision. But look what's in the boat!'

What Ash hadn't noticed, and most shocking of all, was that there was a dead man sitting at each oar.

Their skin had turned black and leathery, stretched tight over their skeletons. Most of their eyes were shut and their mouths hung slightly open. They wore helmets and the black tunics Arthur had seen in his vision. One man sat apart from the rest, at the bow, facing the Jormungand. He alone wore a bronze helmet while the others all wore leather ones. Apart from that, the helmets were of an identical design, with rounded tops and a long strip covering the bridge of the nose. The symbol of the World Serpent clinging to the tree adorned the front of each helmet, to protect the soldiers from the dangers of the Jormungand.

'They're really well preserved,' Ash said. 'Who do you think they were?'

'They're the hundred men who guarded the Jormungand,' Will explained. 'They died guarding it.'

'What's that?' Max asked. He was pointing to a stone table near the boat. In fact, it wasn't a table, Arthur realised as he approached it: it was an altar. A helmet, tunic, trousers and sandals were arranged on it in the shape of a man. These were all identical to the ones the soldiers in the boat wore. Gloves stood in for hands and one of the gloves was wrapped around a large iron hammer, like a hand clutching it. The hammer's head was curved downward slightly on top, almost like a boomerang. Runes were carved into the iron but none that Arthur recognised. The wooden handle the head was attached to was quite short, barely long enough for a grown man to grip, and wrapped tightly in fine twine. There was nothing in the least bit attractive about it, but Arthur just couldn't help reaching out and touching it.

Flash!

The green flash of light was brighter than any of the ones he'd experienced before – in the water or when Will had touched the pendant – forcing him to shut his eyes. When he opened them, he found himself standing at the bus stop near his house. Suddenly he saw Max running towards him, kicking his football as always. But coming after him was none other than Arthur himself! Ash was beside the other Arthur, strolling slowly. They all seemed blissfully unaware that there were two versions of Arthur at the bus stop. In fact, if Max didn't watch out, he was going to run straight into him. Arthur braced himself for the collision, but then something even stranger happened – Max ran right through him as if he wasn't there. Then the other Arthur and Ash arrived and walked right through him too.

Arthur suddenly realised that what he was seeing wasn't really happening. It was some kind of memory. It appeared to be a memory of his first day at Belmont. The bus was approaching at the end of the road and Max was gloating that he'd won the race to the bus stop. Will was crossing the road towards them.

'Hi,' he said. His voice reverberated, as if the sound was really echoing though Arthur's mind. He supposed it was.

But from this point on the scene was not how Arthur remembered it.

'Hello,' said Ash. She seemed irritated. 'I'm sorry but do I know you?'

Will planted his arm around her shoulders. Ash, Max and the other Arthur all appeared confused and looked at Will suspiciously.

'Oh,' he said, 'not now you don't. But you will.

Because, you see, I'm one of your best friends. Have been for years. And little Max, you adore me. Now, I'm going to walk away. I'll be back in a minute. And you're going to introduce me to Arthur here.' He turned to cross back over the road.

'And another thing,' he said, stopping in the middle of the road and turning around, 'you'll also forget that I was just here when I click my fingers.' And with that, he clicked them.

Flash!

Back in the cavern now and back in reality, Arthur took his hand off the strange hammer. He turned to look at Will, who was examining the Jormungand's face more closely. Max was near him, standing slightly away from the creature. Will rubbed his hand tenderly across one of the World Serpent's closed eyelids. He seemed lost in thought but eventually looked up to see Arthur staring at him.

'Arthur?' he said. 'Is something wrong?'

'You lied to us,' Arthur accused him.

'Well,' said Will, a grin forming on his face, 'it is in my nature.'

CHAPTER EIGHTEEN

'What do you mean he lied to us?' Ash asked from where she stood next to the altar.

'He's been lying since the first time we met him,' Arthur explained, not taking his eyes off Will, who kept still, just grinning that grin. 'You thought you knew him, Ash, but you didn't. He hypnotised you somehow. He tricked you into thinking you were friends. He tricked us all. And then he made us forget. He's not really Will – in fact, there is no Will.'

'Oh, very good!' cried the boy they'd known as Will, clapping his hands. 'How did you work that out?' He then spotted the hammer on the stone altar behind Arthur. 'Oh, you touched the war hammer, didn't you?' That hammer has caused me a lot of hardship over the years.' In one swift movement, he took off his backpack and threw it against the far wall of the cavern. It landed with a heavy thud that resounded around the cavern.

'What are you doing?' cried Arthur, startled.

'Don't worry, Artie. I'm not doing anything.'

'I don't get it,' Ash murmured, 'when did he hypnotise us?'

'Remember my first day at school, when we walked to the bus stop together?' Arthur said. 'How it felt like time had skipped forward a minute? Well it didn't skip forward. Will hypnotised us and made us forget that minute. He lied about everything: the whole story about his father and their family, why the pendant blasted near him, who he actually is – everything!'

Ash turned to face Will. 'Max, come over here,' she said.

As Max started towards his sister, Will grabbed him by the back of his shirt.

'Hey, let me go!' Max cried.

'Let you go?' Will said menacingly. '*Let you go?*' He

picked Max up by the collar as if he weighed no more than a feather pillow and held him out at arm's length. 'Will I let him go, Ash?'

'He's only a child, Will. Please, just put him down.'

'Oh, he *is* just a child,' Will agreed as if he'd only become informed of the fact, 'but then that's my child.' He pointed to the Jormungand with his free hand. 'That's my child. And look how they locked him up down here!' He shook Max violently as he spoke, then threw him against the Jormungand. When he landed with a thud on the ground, Max went to run to Ash but Will pointed at him, warning him, '*Stay where you are!* All of you. Nobody move.'

The sound of his voice froze them all in place.

'So who are you really?' Ash asked, her own voice trembling.

'Oh, haven't you worked it out yet, Ash?' His voice turned deep and raspy when he spoke the next words. 'Let me make it simple for you.' A lime-green light suddenly poured out of Will's eyes, enveloping him. Blazing streaks swirled around him, from his ankles all the way up to his head. When the light eventually faded, Will was no longer there. He had been transformed into a tall, blonde woman in a slinky red dress.

'Maybe I'm the woman who stole a file that helped her find the new head engineer, Joe Quinn, and his son, Arthur,' the woman said in the same croaky voice. The green light covered her again. When it dispersed this time, Will was back, wearing his school uniform.

'Or maybe, I'm the young boy, Will Doyle, who befriended Arthur Quinn so that he'd help him find a giant serpent underground.' The green aura came and went again. This time, Will had become a fully grown young man, with glorious flowing blond hair and a neatly trimmed beard. He was wearing an olive green tunic and golden crown.

'Perhaps,' rasped the man, 'you'd prefer to see me in my former glory. Before I was bound in a cave under Dublin and tortured for a thousand years. Or perhaps you'd like to see me as I am now. In my true form.'

The emerald light oozed from his eyes once more, covering every inch of his body. When it faded for the last time, the young man had metamorphosed into an older, more haggard version of himself. His hair was lank and greasy, his beard bushy. The skin on his face was red and blotchy, tiny scars blistering its surface. He was dressed completely in black, with the heavy black boots Arthur had seen in the playhouse not so long ago.

'Let me introduce myself properly,' said the person they'd come to know as Will. 'I am the Father of Lies, the Trickster God, the God of Mischief, the Lie-smith. I am Loki.' The now-familiar grin spread across his face, teeth bared threateningly. 'Surprised?'

As Loki was going through his various transformations, Arthur was looking around frantically trying to figure out what to do. He spotted the canvas bag of dynamite still by the entrance to the cavern. He had a sudden thought. If he could just distract Loki enough, he might be able to spill the explosives into the water outside, making them useless. He hadn't worked out why yet, but he knew that the dynamite had to be important to Loki's scheme, considering he was the one who had suggested bringing it here in the first place. Somehow he had to get to the bag before Loki could stop him.

'Why are you doing all this?' asked Arthur, hoping to keep the Trickster God talking long enough to put his plan into action. If there was one part of Loki that had seeped through his Will-disguise, it was that he clearly loved to brag.

'Oh, so many reasons!' laughed Loki. 'For starters, I'd like to repay the gods who locked me up in that cave for what they did – I want to see them suffer just as I suffered.'

'I saw that,' Arthur put in. 'I saw what the gods did. How they punished you. No one should have to endure that sort of pain. But now's your chance to make amends, to –'

'Shut up!' yelled Loki, suddenly angry. 'I don't want your pity! Or to make amends.' He drew a deep breath, calming himself and then continued, 'You know, my useless human wife died after sixty years. Even though Odin, in his infinite wisdom, took away all her appetites, she eventually died of old age. She couldn't empty the pan of venom after that. So the venom dripped on me for a thousand years. You can't know what it was like. You'll never know. The pain was *excruciating*. Until it ended a few weeks ago. The drilling for the Metro shook loose a piece of rock that killed the snake. After a while, when the pain had gone and my strength started to return, I was able to make my escape.'

'Then what?' Arthur asked, inching towards the entrance.

'Well, I knew I'd need help finding and releasing the Jormungand. The Vikings wouldn't have made it easy for me. They made pendants to protect themselves: some with the Jormungand on them, like the one you found, and some with my face. Each one had a clever built-in security system. Every time I'd touch it, it would blast me away. There was no way I'd have been able to use it as a key. But not only that, I couldn't see the pendant until you found it, Arthur. I'd spent days down here by myself looking for the entrance or the key, both hidden to me by magic. But you found it for me, Arthur. You were the perfect choice. You were new in town and didn't know anyone – easy to befriend, easier to manipulate. You could get access to the site through your father, who was too distracted with his new, important job to realise you were sneaking about. And, best of all, you were a child. I've always found that children are far more willing to go on crazy, dangerous adventures than their parents.' He turned to Max, who hadn't moved from his spot lying against the World Serpent. 'Isn't that right, little Maxie?'

When Loki looked away, Arthur took another long stride towards the bag. Ash noticed and looked questioningly at him. He nodded towards the dynamite. Ash caught on to his plan quickly.

'That's why you kept trying to convince us to come back down here,' Ash said, taking up the conversation to distract Loki's attention from Arthur's progress. 'To find the entrance.'

'Of course. You were very hard to convince at first. Until you had a bit more motive after Daddy Quinn was attacked.' At this, he laughed heartily, holding his belly as he did. 'Now that was one of my favourite parts: the sound of Daddy's bones snapping and the stench of his blood.'

'You must be very proud,' Ash said bitterly, watching Arthur out of the corner of her eye. He was still inching towards the bag, but now there was an expression of anger all over his face.

'Oh, I am!' Loki giggled.

'But how do you think you're going to wake up the Jormungand? It's been asleep for a thousand years.'

'Look around you, Ash. There's a boat and a giant flying sea serpent. What's missing from this picture?'

She shook her head slowly. Loki turned to Max and asked him the same question.

'There's no water,' he answered sheepishly.

'From the mouths of babes,' mused Loki to himself, then turned triumphantly back to Ash. 'He's *exactly* right! There's no water. And that's all I need to awaken the World Serpent. It came from the water so that's all I need to restore it. It's like the final magic ingredient. Some water. Well, a lot of water actually. It needs to be submerged.'

'So what are you going to do now?' she asked, still watching Arthur out of the corner of her eye. 'Are you going to let us go?'

'Let you go? As if! But what will I do *right now*? Hmm …' Loki rubbed his bristly chin as if he really hadn't thought about it before. He pointed to the wall he'd dropped his backpack beside. 'Through that wall is the River Liffey. The Liffey! Ha! The Vikings thought they were so smart burying the Jormungand here, in this nice dry cavern. Of course, they could never have imagined something like dynamite. So clever, you humans sometimes. So good at coming up with ways to destroy each other,' he sneered. 'But not as clever as me. Imagine! The Liffey, so conveniently placed next to my sleeping child. All it will take is a little explosion and then he will sleep no more. And when he awakens people will just be starting to get up, getting ready to go to work or school, living their pathetic little lives with no idea of what is to come. Because what I'm going to do *right now* is free the Jormungand and wreak havoc on Ireland, then on the world.' His voice, which had been increasing in volume as his excitement grew, rose to a shriek. 'The total destruction of civilisation. It's going to be my best trick yet.'

'Not as good as this one!' cried Arthur suddenly, as he kicked the bag out of the entrance to the cave. They all heard the sticks of dynamite fall straight into the water, quickly becoming soaked and useless.

'Oh no!' screamed Loki, collapsing to his knees. He pounded the floor, wailing at the top of his lungs. 'Nooooo! Why, oh why, oh why? My plan is foiled! If it wasn't for you pesky kids I'd have gotten away with it too. My poor plan is – bwah hah ha ha ha!' The cry turned into a guffaw. Tears really were running down Loki's face – tears of laughter. He got to his feet.

'Oh, Arthur,' he said shaking his head, as if he was disappointed. 'Oh, Arthur, Arthur, Arthur … you really thought that would work? Get back over by the altar. You and Ash stand together.'

Arthur looked at the soaking sticks of dynamite once more, then did as he was told. Ash saw the look of worry in his eyes. This time it was her turn to squeeze his hand.

'I have, of course, a back-up plan,' Loki explained. He picked up his backpack at the wall and turned it over, emptying it. A strange-looking device fell out. It essentially consisted of several red sticks of dynamite attached to a ticking analogue alarm clock. 'I stole the dynamite when I attacked your dad, Arthur. Then it was very easy to find directions to make a bomb on this internet thing you have. Oh, look at that!' He pointed to the time on the clock. 'We're just in time for the fireworks. It's going to be like New Year's Eve in here any second!'

He took one lunging step away from the wall and the bomb.

'*Three!*' he proclaimed dramatically.

Max shuffled further down along the Jormungand. He squeezed himself into a curve of the serpent's body and covered his head.

'*Two!*' cried Loki, taking another step.

Arthur and Ash crawled underneath the altar and ducked down, covering their heads.

'*One!*'

CHAPTER NINETEEN

The bomb blasted a hole outwards in the wall behind Loki. The force of the explosion sent him flying to the ground, laughing maniacally as he went. He turned around just in time to see an enormous wave of water rush through the hole. He scrambled to his feet – the water up to his knees already – and ran towards Max.

As soon as the dynamite had gone off, Max had dashed to the boat and tried to climb in, but he was far too short to reach the edge. Loki grabbed him by the back of his jacket and picked him up so that their faces were level.

'You're coming with me, Maxie,' he sneered. 'I always thought you'd make a useful hostage!'

Arthur and Ash, meanwhile, were trapped on top of the altar which they'd mounted after the explosion. The water had nearly reached the top already, making it feel less like an altar and more like a desert island.

With the strong tide flowing in, the hole in the wall grew larger as the force of the water cracked it further. More and more pieces of rock crumbled and fell as if they'd never been solid to begin with. The water in the cavern was almost in line with the River Liffey through the hole and it kept rising, but more slowly now. The sky was grey outside, as the pale October sun rose and the city slowly started to wake.

The Jormungand began to stir as Loki pushed Max up onto the serpent's back. Loki then clambered up himself, positioning himself behind Max against one of the Jormungand's dorsal fins. The water had risen enough to cover the beast's mouth. Arthur saw its tail flicker over and past the end of the boat, its claws twitching under the water. The flood washed against the eyes of the Jormungand. And, with that, they shot open.

Loki and Max had to hold onto the fins tightly as the Jormungand's massive head lifted off the ground.

It opened its mouth – two sabre-toothed fangs were embedded in the top lip while a fork-tipped tongue flicked out, tasting the air. It roared triumphantly, an ear-piercing screech like chalk on a blackboard.

'Ha ha!' shrieked Loki. 'It's alive! It's alive!'

'*Help!*' Max screamed, reaching out towards Ash and Arthur. 'Ash, help me!'

'Will – I mean, Loki, please,' Ash begged from their stone island, 'please let him go.' She could feel tears running down her cheeks.

'Oh, don't worry, Ash. We're going. But you're staying here. To die.' He tapped the Jormungand on the head and whispered something they couldn't understand. His eyes shone green again and he transformed back into his Will-disguise. 'Arthur, Ash, it was nice knowing you. Well, actually, on second thoughts, it wasn't really. Bye bye!'

The serpent shot out through the hole in the wall, Loki and Max clinging on for dear life. As it passed Ash and Arthur, the end of its tail swung out and whacked them, sending them flying towards the entrance they'd come in. They landed in the water with a splash, the breath knocked out of them. The water was now up to their chests and they managed to struggle to their feet just as the Jormungand's tail flicked out of the cavern. It knocked off some more rock on the way, starting a further avalanche of stones. The whole cavern was now shaking and rocks were falling from the ceiling.

Arthur looked around at Ash just in time to see the door to the entrance sliding shut. Without another thought, he pushed Ash as hard as he could, sending her toppling back through the gap just before it closed for good.

'Arthur!' She banged on the other side. 'Arthur! Get out of there quick! Swim out! There'll be another cave-in!'

A huge wave was rushing into the cavern now, caused by the serpent's rush into the Liffey outside. The water level rose drastically and the wave swept Arthur away from the entrance back towards the Viking longboat. Toppling head over heels in the icy cold water, he was trying to work out which way was up when he spotted the hammer lying on the ground below him. Loki had not liked the hammer and Arthur had an idea that it could be useful in fighting him. He swam down to pick it up.

It was pure dead weight and the slippery footing underneath wasn't helping as Arthur tried to push himself up towards the surface. He managed to get the hammer off the ground, clutching it to his chest, but as he looked up towards the surface of the water he saw that a rock the size of a fist had come loose from the ceiling and was falling straight towards him. He was so busy trying to move out of its way, he didn't even feel it hitting him on the forehead, and all he saw was blackness as he fell unconscious and drifted towards the bottom of the cavern.

Loki and Max held their breath as the Jormungand dived deep into the River Liffey. Loki knew exactly how the serpent was feeling. After being in captivity for so many hundreds of years, it felt amazing to be free again, swimming rapidly through the water.

Max just held on for dear life, his eyes and mouth shut tightly. He didn't know how to swim and he'd always looked at deep water like this with fear. Now he was really wishing he'd just stayed in bed instead of following the others.

The World Serpent careened upwards and flew straight out of the water and into the sky. Up, up and up it soared, water dripping off its sleek body back into the river. Their ears popped as they shot even higher. Max squinted out of one eye, saw how high they were and shut it again. The air was thin at this height so he concentrated on breathing instead.

Loki admired the view. Dublin city. The sun rising in the east over the port and glinting off the expensive glass buildings in the financial district. The older buildings on this side of the city so rich in history, the expansive river below them. He could see a few buses and cars along the quays, some of which ground to a halt as passengers craned their necks to watch the flying serpent, rubbing their eyes as if to wake themselves from a dream. So much to destroy, so much to wipe out. Devastation really was a joyous thing.

With the lack of quality oxygen Max was feeling light-headed. He couldn't keep his grip on the fin any more and slipped off the side, screaming. The ground rushed quickly towards him. Suddenly the Jormungand dived back around, catching him as he plummeted. This time Loki held on to Max as they continued flying over the river.

'Hold tight, Maxie,' he said. 'We don't want you to die. Well, not just yet.'

�֍✕✕✕✕✕

Ash banged her fist on the stone entrance a few more times before giving up.

'Arthur!' she shouted in over the rush of the water. 'I hope you can hear me. I need to go and help Max. I'm sorry. But I'll come back for you. Or I'll send someone back. Don't worry! I just need to save my brother.' There was no response. 'Arthur, can you hear me?' Still no answer. She could only hope that he'd managed to swim out of the cavern in time.

She looked at her watch. It was just after seven

o'clock and the water in the tunnel hadn't started rising yet. She darted back the way they'd come earlier, passing the warning carvings on the wall. If only we'd listened to those warnings, Ash thought to herself.

She didn't want to risk running the whole way back to where they'd come in at the Metro tunnel. Apart from the shortage of time, she was worried that the longer she stayed underground, the higher the chance of drowning would be. When she reached the fork, she took the small tunnel to the left. Eventually she came to the archway they'd escaped through when they'd almost drowned. The grate hadn't been replaced yet, thankfully. The water in the Liffey wasn't as high at this point as it had been the last time. There was a good five-foot drop from the tunnel down to the river. She looked out and to the side. A few feet away, an iron ladder was attached to the wall which led up to street level. She put her arm out, trying to reach it, but didn't come close. A small ledge ran at the height of the tunnel the whole way along the wall. It barely protruded three inches and was covered in slippery-looking gunk, but Ash knew it was her only option.

She looked up to her right and saw the black silhouette of the Jormungand soaring against the sky. If she hadn't known about the terror it would unleash on the world, she would have thought it looked pretty up there. Suddenly a small figure fell off its back, dropping rapidly towards the ground.

'Max!' she cried in fear.

As the serpent swooped down and caught Max, she let out a sigh of relief, then steadied herself and stepped out onto the ledge. Her foot slipped almost instantly. She clutched at the wall to stop herself falling, then tried again, forcing all of her weight onto her tiptoes. She faced the wall, clinging to it, and slid along the ledge inch by inch. The black-green gunk on the ledge collected between her feet, making the journey even more treacherous. When she was within reach of the ladder, she grabbed it and her feet lurched straight out from under her. Holding on with all her strength, she scrabbled with her feet until she got them onto the lowest rung and then climbed quickly up to the road.

Traffic was at a total standstill. Most drivers and

passengers had clambered out to witness the strange creature in the sky and were standing in the road, staring upwards and pointing. None of them even noticed her climbing up from the river.

'Get in your cars,' Ash said to the people nearest her.

'What do you think it is?' a nearby driver said to his passenger, never taking his eyes off the Jormungand.

'Just get in your cars!' Ash shouted it this time. 'All of you! Get in and drive away. It's dangerous. Go somewhere safe.'

Everyone standing in the road ignored her. 'Look,' said a truck driver, pointing at the serpent. 'It's going towards O'Connell Street.'

O'Connell Street: the busiest street in Dublin. The perfect place for the Jormungand to start its destruction, Ash realised grimly. She left the spectators in the road and ran over the Ha'penny Bridge, turning right and heading towards O'Connell Street as fast as she could go.

O'Connell Street is the main thoroughfare running

through the centre of Dublin. Flanked on either side by tall buildings of historical significance, shops and restaurants, it has a wide pedestrian pavement along the centre. Halfway down this pedestrian island is the Millennium Spire, a four-hundred-foot-tall spike constructed of shiny steel. The monument usually causes tourists to look skyward, but at this time of the morning O'Connell Street was still fairly quiet, with mostly just workers going to their early shifts. A florist's stall with a canvas roof was setting up for business by the Spire, next to a newspaper vendor. A few taxis and buses were moving up and down each side of the street. Most of the people on the street had lived in Dublin for years and none of them thought to look upwards.

When Ash turned on to O'Connell Street, the first thing she noticed was the Jormungand wrapped around the top half of the Spire. She could just about make out Loki and Max, still clinging to one of the fins. The serpent seemed to be relaxing, watching the people going about their business, itself going largely unnoticed.

Ash wondered what it was doing just sitting there but was relieved it hadn't yet attacked anyone.

She raced down the street, waving at pedestrians and urging them to get indoors. They looked at her like she was out of her mind but this didn't put her off.

'Please!' she begged. 'Get inside somewhere. It's dangerous! Look up – look at the Spire!'

'Yeah, whatever,' one passer-by said cynically.

'No, actually, look,' said another one who had done what Ash asked. 'What is that thing?'

'It's a –' Ash started. Just then Loki pointed at her from atop the serpent. The Jormungand saw her, then uncoiled from the monument and launched itself towards Ash and the people near her. It screeched its ear-piercing call as it dived through the air.

Ash and the others turned to the nearest building. It was a large bookshop that hadn't opened for business for the day yet. Although the glass entrance doors were still locked, the steel shutters were up and they could see staff getting the place ready. By the looks of things they'd just taken in the day's newspapers and were stacking them on their shelves. Ash and the others outside banged on the doors.

One staff member looked up from his sweeping and shook his head apologetically. 'We're not open yet,' he said.

Ash kept pounding. She turned around and saw that the Jormungand had landed on the ground in the middle of the road. It hadn't taken any notice of the light traffic still moving down the street. The driver of a lorry had no time to swerve: the vehicle crashed into the serpent's side, sending the beast rolling onto its back. Loki and Max toppled backwards and landed on the tarmac with a thud. Before Max could even think of making an escape, Loki grabbed hold of him again. Meanwhile, the Jormungand was writhing about on its spine, struggling to turn the right way up. Ash turned her attention back to the bookshop.

'Please, please let us in!' she cried.

The bookseller kept shaking his head. He walked towards the doors, thinking they couldn't hear him. 'I told you already, we're not –' Then he saw the Jormungand behind the people outside. It had managed to right itself, but was standing shaking its head, still stunned from the impact of the lorry. The driver – along with several others – had abandoned his vehicle and joined the crowd at the bookshop.

'Hurry up!' Loki shouted at the serpent from where he stood, with a tight grip on Max. 'They're going to get away!'

The Jormungand finally turned back towards the people on the bookshop steps and roared.

As the sound echoed around the street, the bookseller swiftly unhooked a large loop of keys from his belt. He fumbled with the key-ring, dropping it to the floor. Ash and the others groaned and she looked over her shoulder at the Jormungand, which was licking its lips in anticipation of the meal to come, as if it was toying with its food. It started moving quickly towards them, unhindered by its tiny legs.

'Come on, come on!' Ash urged the bookseller. He'd retrieved the loop from the ground and was trying key after key in the lock. Suddenly there was a click. He pulled the doors open triumphantly and everyone piled in, the weight of all the bodies pressing forward sending them crashing to the floor. Quickly the bookseller pulled down the shutters, locked them and then shut the inner doors for extra protection, just as the serpent slammed its head against the steel.

Ash sat up, catching her breath. She looked around her at the grateful people. They were safe. For the moment at least. But Max was still trapped outside with Loki.

※※※※※

Arthur came to with a dull throbbing in his forehead and found he was flat on his back staring at the ceiling of the cavern. He touched his hand to the throbbing spot to find a small lump. It stung to the touch although he was thankful to see that there was no blood on his hand when he took it away and held it in front of his eyes.

Where am I, he wondered to himself. He reached out around him. He was on dry land at least, and as he explored further he realised that he was lying on a wooden floor. With a groan he struggled upright. He quickly saw that he was in the Viking boat, which was now bobbing calmly on the surface of the water in the cavern. What's more, he was surrounded by the group of dead Viking soldiers. Only they weren't quite dead any more. They were moving. And one of them was steadily advancing towards him, carrying the strange iron hammer raised in his hands.

CHAPTER TWENTY

After a few more futile attempts to break into the bookshop, the Jormungand gave up.

'Save your energy, my child,' Ash heard Loki shout to the Jormungand. 'You've been asleep for hundreds of years. It would take anyone a while to get their strength back. You're not restored to your full power yet. When you are, those shutters will be like mere paper to you.' The terrified people in the shop breathed a sigh of relief as they heard the beast walk away, its claws scratching the pavement.

'Is there anywhere we can see out?' someone asked the staff member who'd opened the door for them.

'The windows on the third floor are quite large,'

he said. 'You'll get a good view of the whole street up there.' The people who'd been outside and most of the staff members took off, running up the steps of the escalator, which had not been started yet, two at a time. Ash looked at their saviour. He was in his early twenties with three piercings in each ear.

'Thanks for letting everyone in,' Ash said, 'but you have to let me back out now.'

'What? Are you crazy?'

'No. You just have to let me out.' She thought of Max. 'My brother's out there. Please. Open the shutters.'

'No way. I don't care if it sounds like it's gone. That thing could get in here and kill us all. Or if you go out, it could kill you. There's no way I'm letting a kid like you go out into the street to face that thing! Why don't you come upstairs? At least that way you can see what's going on.'

Ash thought about it for a moment, but quickly realised that just as Max was trapped outside, she was trapped in the shop. She knew from his tone of voice there was no convincing the bookseller to let her out and, since he was much bigger than her, there was no way she could force him to open the door. As much as Arthur had been trapped in the cavern, she was trapped in here. Worried and frustrated, she conceded and followed him upstairs.

'What is that thing anyway?' he asked on the way up.

'You don't want to know,' she replied grimly.

❋❋❋❋❋

When the serpent, Loki and Max got back to the Spire, the Jormungand slumped to the ground with a raspy sigh. Loki rubbed the side of its face lovingly.

'Aw,' he said, 'are you tired from banging your head on that door? Poor Jormungand. You know, you may be my largest child, you may be my oldest child, but you're certainly not my smartest.' The serpent seemed oblivious to the insult. It was watching the people still on the street. They were running away in all directions, screaming and yelling, heading for any shelter they could find. If the Jormungand had had more energy he would have devoured all of them in one swift flight.

But his father was right: best to conserve what energy he had for the moment.

'Will?' said Max's voice shyly. 'I want to go home.'

Loki turned to him in disgust. 'Are you stupid or something? Don't you get it yet? I'm not Will.'

'You look like Will.'

'There is no Will. There never was. I'm Loki.'

He momentarily transformed to the ancient and scarred Loki form.

'See?' he asked. Then he changed back to Will.

Max couldn't hold it in any more. What with the swim through the water and the terrifying flight above the city and Will not being real, he'd had enough. He started to cry.

'Oh, do stop crying, Max. Grow up! You should try to enjoy yourself.' At this Max tried to halt his tears. Loki stooped and put an arm around the boy. 'You know, one day, when you're old, if you're still alive – which, let's be honest, is looking less and less likely – people might ask each other where they were on the day the world was destroyed. And you'll have the pleasure of telling them that you were standing next to Loki the Trickster himself. Won't that be nice?'

At this, Max only cried harder.

※※※※

The dead man advanced slowly on Arthur. His leathery dark-brown skin stretched over his skeletal form. His cheekbones were high and sharp and his brow was prominent, which caused his black eyes to appear even more sunken than they actually were. His mouth was slightly open, displaying cracked yellow teeth. There was very little hair left of his beard. From the bronze helmet he was wearing, Arthur recognised him as the dead Viking who had been sitting staring at the Jormungand from the bow of the boat. As he walked forward, he stretched the hammer out towards Arthur, groaning deeply.

'Please, don't hurt me,' Arthur said, shielding his head and face with his arms. 'I need to get out of here and help my friends.'

The dead man stopped and looked at the others in confusion. A couple of them shrugged their shoulders, silently. The man with the hammer moved forward again. He made a guttural, croaky sound. Even though it sounded ugly, Arthur detected no sense of a threat. He looked up at the dead man and realised that he wasn't going to hit him with the hammer. In fact, he seemed to be offering it to Arthur.

'You're giving this to me?' Arthur asked. He pointed to the outstretched hammer and then to himself.

The man grunted again, thrusting the weapon forwards as if to emphasise the point. Arthur accepted the gift. Strangely, it didn't feel as heavy in his hands as it had done before. It almost felt like it belonged in his grasp.

'Thank you,' he said. Using the hammer as a small crutch, Arthur got to his feet.

'Did you save me?' he asked, looking around him at the men. 'Did you pull me out of the water?' They looked confused then grunted in a puzzled way. 'I guess you can't understand me, huh?' Just then he remembered the pendant. He took it out of his pocket and hung it around his neck. It momentarily glowed green then faded.

'Do you understand me now?' Arthur said. The dead men smiled and nodded frantically. A series of excited throaty sounds came out of their mouths.

'Can you speak?' he asked. They shook their heads. 'I guess being dead for a thousand years would mess up your vocal cords a bit. Okay, grunt once for yes and twice for no. Understand?'

The man with the bronze helmet – Arthur thought of him as their leader – grunted once.

'Great. So you rescued me from the water?'

The leader grunted again.

'And the hammer?' At this they all nodded frantically again. 'And this hammer's very important?' They nodded even more, all of them grunting loudly.

Arthur walked through the men to the end of the boat. They parted to let him explore. Shields, armour and weapons were scattered about. He stood for a moment at the end of the boat, looking out through the hole to the Liffey, thinking. When he'd worked out what was going on, he turned back to face the dead men.

'You're the hundred men that were guarding the Jormungand, right?' he said. The leader groaned once but dropped his head, as if he was ashamed of the job they'd done.

'But you came back to life because it escaped? Like a back-up plan?' As the leader grunted once, the men nodded.

'That's brilliant. Bet Loki didn't see that one coming. I'm Arthur, by the way.'

'Ar-kkkrrr,' the leader croaked. He slapped his own chest. 'Be-yr-n.'

'Be-yr-n?' Arthur repeated. 'You're Be-yr-n?'

The leader nodded and smiled.

'Oh, I get it now! Like Bjorn. Your name is Bjorn?'

Bjorn bowed his head with a grin.

Arthur pointed straight at Bjorn. 'So I guess you're in charge, Bjorn? Like their general?' At this, Bjorn shook his head and grunted twice. He pointed to Arthur. 'I'm the general?' The men all nodded.

Then, one by one, all the other soldiers fell to one knee. They took off their helmets and bowed their heads towards Arthur in deep respect. He looked to Bjorn, who simply grimaced back in what Arthur took to be an attempt at a smile.

'Well then,' Arthur announced, walking to the bow of the boat, then turning to face the Vikings. 'Last time it took Thor and the gods to stop Loki's madness. If my vision was correct, they can't help us this time. But my friends are out there with Loki and we have to save them and stop him. I don't know if we'll be able to. But we have to try.'

CHAPTER TWENTY-ONE

Watching the empty street from a third-floor window of the bookshop, the helpful staff member said, 'There are some kids out there. See? On the giant snake: two boys by the looks of it.'

The refugees were clustered around the large windows, peering out and fogging up the glass with their breath. The Jormungand had wound itself back around the Spire, and Loki and Max were resting on one of the head fins.

'That's my brother,' Ash said. 'That's why you need to let me out.'

'I'm not letting you out. Which one is your brother? The blond kid?'

'No,' she replied. 'The blond one is ... Never mind, you'd never believe me anyway.'

'I wouldn't have believed you an hour ago if you'd told me I'd be seeing a hundred-foot-long snake terrorising the city. But my eyes aren't lying to me. So tell me, who's the blond kid?'

Ash took a deep breath and began, 'He's the ancient Viking god Loki, the Trickster God, who's been held captive under Dublin for more than a millennium and now plans on destroying the entire world for his revenge. That giant snake thing is his child.'

The shop assistant just looked at Ash for a minute, gobsmacked. 'Tch!' he said, rolling his eyes. 'Yeah, right!'

'I told you you wouldn't believe me,' said Ash, turning back to the window just in time to see a helicopter pass by as it flew towards the Jormungand.

�֎֎֎֎֎

Loki heard the helicopter approaching as he lay back on the serpent's fin. The propellers chopped at the air, making a *fwp-fwp* sound. It flew from the south, the direction of the Liffey, and hovered in the centre of the street at roughly the same height as the buildings. It was white with a fluorescent yellow stripe edged with blue painted down the sides.

'Uh oh,' Loki remarked sarcastically to Max, 'here comes the cavalry.'

The helicopter hung in the air in front of them, the rush of wind from the propellers making the Spire sway. Max clung on to Loki's waist, afraid of falling again.

'Attention!' a voice boomed from the megaphone attached to the side of the helicopter. 'This is the Garda Síochána! Please remove yourself and your … eh … giant snake … eh … whatever that thing is from the Spire. Immediately.'

'And what if we don't?' Loki shouted back, using his magic to project his voice so it could be heard over the noise of the helicopter's engine.

'Well, then we'll be forced to remove you by … eh … extreme measures!'

Loki patted the side of the Jormungand's massive head.

'Oh puh-leese,' he said to it. 'Who do they think they are? Even at your weakest you could dispose of that flying tin can easily. In fact, I think it's time to unleash our secret weapon.' He leaned closer to the Jormungand and kissed the top of its skull. 'Now, let's show them what you've got.'

With that command, the beast opened its vicious jaws and roared. Its long, forked tongue flickered in the air and huge drops of spittle flew out of its mouth and landed on the window of the helicopter. The force of the air being expelled from the Jormungand's lungs was so great that the helicopter careened backwards, flipping over and over in the air.

The screech ended as the Jormungand ran out of breath. Then it inhaled, looked up to the sky and roared once more. This time, green rays of light shot out of its mouth, as if propelled by the noise itself. The green light soaked into the clouds, turning them a sickly moss green.

Meanwhile, the garda pilot had completely lost control of his vehicle. As the 'flying tin can' tumbled towards the street below, the pilot and co-pilot flung themselves out of its doors, crashing onto the pavement with heavy thuds. The pilot landed awkwardly and cried out in pain as a bone snapped in his leg. The helicopter itself crashed to the street mere feet away from them and exploded with a bright flash of orange, knocking them backwards. Red flames and black smoke belched high into the sky as Loki laughed feverishly at the destruction.

The Jormungand wailed at the sky once more as the dark-green clouds sank closer to the earth.

The dead army rowed the boat through the hole in the wall and out onto the River Liffey. The sail just about cleared the crumbling upper part of the gap. Arthur had changed out of his soaking clothes and into a black tunic and brown trousers that one of the Vikings had handed him. The pendant pulsated green on his chest.

'It's very quiet,' he remarked to Bjorn by his side as they sailed the boat towards O'Connell Bridge. Just then a garda helicopter flew over the bridge in the direction of the Spire. From his position on the boat, Arthur couldn't see what happened but he certainly could hear the roar of the Jormungand and the loud blast that followed shortly afterwards as the helicopter hit the ground and exploded. Arthur watched in awe as thick black smoke rose over the buildings. Then he noticed green rays shooting skywards into the clouds now gathering over that part of the city – thick clouds that looked like they were full of heavy rain. But they were also a deep green, with flashes of light moving through them like shots of electricity, and they were quickly spreading as far as the eye could see.

He turned to Bjorn – he now thought of him as his second-in-command – and said, 'We have to hurry. I just hope we're not already too late.'

The Jormungand crawled back down the length of the Spire towards the smoking wreckage. The fire had already burnt itself out, but a thick cloud of dense smoke still rose from the ashes. When the serpent reached the ground, Loki slid off, pulling Max with him. The Jormungand looked around and then focused its gaze on the injured pilot lying on the road. His broken leg was sticking out at a strange angle in front of him and the Jormungand began to advance on him, slithering along the ground on its belly rather than walking on its tiny legs. The pilot started to drag himself backwards using his arms and pushing with his good leg, but the monster was gaining on him quickly. The co-pilot, who had not hurt himself too badly in the jump from the helicopter, raced up to the pilot and grabbed him under the arms, lifting him onto his good leg. The two quickly hobbled to the relative safety of a nearby café. The door shut tightly behind them and the occupants looked fearfully out the window.

'Ha ha!' guffawed Loki. 'Run away, little piggies, run away. Then we'll huff and we'll puff and we'll blow your house –'

He was cut off when a drop of water landed beside him. Max jumped back from the puddle it made. It was more than an ordinary drop – it was huge, the size of an average bucketful. When it hit the ground, it burst with a loud *thwump*.

Loki looked up at the green clouds.

'It's starting,' he said to himself quietly, almost in awe. More giant drops fell around them. He turned on the spot, waving his arms jubilantly. 'It's *starting*!'

He picked up Max and swung him around. 'It's starting, Maxie! The end of the world!'

Before Max could reply, Loki leaped onto the World Serpent's back, pulling Max along with him. They were in the air again in seconds and the Jormungand once more wrapped itself around the point of the Spire. Loki stood on the top of its head, his arms outstretched triumphantly.

Max peered down at the street below. The few huge drops that had fallen had already soaked the ground. It would only get worse now as the heavens opened. The green clouds showered giant drops onto the city. As Max watched, the streets were flooded in seconds, water rising above the steps of some buildings and slowly starting to seep inside.

The Jormungand roared again. More green light emanated from the scream and soaked into the clouds. Loki was laughing like he never had before.

Arthur had just climbed onto the pavement above the Liffey when the rain started. He was soaked instantly by one giant drop landing next to him. He looked behind him at Bjorn and the others climbing the ladder out of the river. Arthur stretched his hand out to Bjorn to help him over the wall but the Viking shook his head frantically and pointed back at the boat bobbing on the water.

'What is it? What's wrong?'

Bjorn grunted and pointed at the dark clouds then at the river. Arthur saw what he meant now. The water level was already rising drastically with the heavy rain. Although he had been standing on the pavement only a short time, already water lapped around his ankles. At this rate, the river would overflow in a couple of minutes which meant that –

'We can sail down the street to Loki,' Arthur exclaimed, 'and attack from the boat. Great idea!'

Bjorn nodded and grunted to his men. They retreated down the ladder to the rapidly rising boat. The second-in-command waited for Arthur, who had started to follow but then suddenly paused.

'Hold on a second,' Arthur said, running off. He came to the bottom of O'Connell Street. Cautiously, he peeked around the corner. Smoke was rising from the wreckage of the helicopter but the water would soon put that out completely. No one was on the near-flooded street, although he did see several frightened faces staring out at the scene from second- and third-floor windows. The World Serpent was coiled around the top of the Spire, just like it had been wrapped around the tree on his pendant. From this distance, he could just about make out the tiny figures of Loki and Max on its great head. While Max was clinging on for dear life, Loki was standing up, laughing crazily. Arthur ran back to the waiting Viking.

'I have a better plan,' Arthur said. 'Do you see that street back there?' He pointed upriver in the direction of Liffey Street. 'When the water rises enough, sail down that street until you find the cross street that comes out at the Spire – it's called Henry Street, there should be a sign. Then you'll be able to sail at Loki from the other direction: a sneak attack!'

Bjorn grinned in agreement then put his hand out for Arthur.

'No. I'm not going with you. I'll go up O'Connell Street and distract him so he won't see you coming.'

The Viking shook his head, worried for Arthur.

'It's all right, Bjorn. I'll be fine. You go. Sail down Liffey Street as quick as you can. Look – the river is nearly halfway up already!'

With one last look at Arthur, Bjorn climbed down the ladder and onto his boat. As the water continued to rise, he started grunting orders at his dead army. Arthur turned away from them and raced back towards O'Connell Street.

By now the water was up to his shins and approaching his knees quickly. He was astonished at how much rain had fallen in a couple of minutes and even more astonished that the huge drops kept falling.

He peered around the corner onto O'Connell Street again. The street was more flooded now but the Jormungand's position on the Spire hadn't changed. Loki was still laughing at the mayhem, distracted.

Arthur took this chance and ran down the centre of the street – although as the water was up to his waist now it was more a case of wading than running. A handful of tall statues lined the pedestrian area running between the two lines of traffic and Arthur hid behind the first of these. He peered around the edge of the statue. Loki was still distracted by his delight in his own brilliance. This would be a perfect time to make another run for it but the water was chest-high by now and the next statue was too far along to run or wade to quickly.

There was only one thing for it, he realised as he took a deep breath and plunged his head under the water. He couldn't believe that he was actually swimming up O'Connell Street. His head was throbbing from where the rock had hit him in the cavern and his limbs were tired from the exertion but he ignored all that as he focused on the task at hand. One thing he couldn't ignore, though, was that he was running out of breath. He could see a statue just ahead of him in the cloudy water. If he could just make it there …

Seconds later, his fingers touched the stone. He thrust his head out of the water behind the plinth and inhaled air greedily. He found that he was just about able to stand on his tiptoes and keep his head above the water, but that wouldn't last long. As he filled his lungs once more, a movement caught the corner of his eye. From where he was hidden behind the second statue, he was able to see down Middle Abbey Street, which ran perpendicular to O'Connell Street. The movement he saw was the Viking boat – there one second and gone the next – as the warriors rowed strongly up Liffey Street. So far everything was going to plan.

The third statue was the one closest to the Spire. He took a deep breath and swam hastily towards it, hoping and praying that everything would continue to go smoothly.

Loki eventually stopped laughing, to Max's relief.

'Time to address my people, Max,' he said. 'Or should I say "slaves"!'

He stood on the Jormungand's head, steady as a rock.

'People of Dublin!' he cried, his voice carrying magically over the street. 'Welcome to the end of the world. This is how it begins. The floods will come and annihilate you all. Let the flooding begi–'

'*Loki!*'

The voice came from down the street, towards the river, and Loki recognised it instantly. He spotted Arthur standing in front of a statue on a high plinth, managing to avoid the flooded street below. He was wearing the black uniform the corpses had been wearing in the cavern. The pendant hung around his neck and he held the Viking hammer in his right hand.

'Arthur!' cried Max in delight.

'Well lookee who it is,' said Loki in a sing-song voice. 'So you managed to escape, Arthur. Well done. That's commendable. You should be proud.'

'Shut up, Loki!'

The Jormungand screeched at Arthur. Loki calmed it, rubbing the side of its belly.

'Oh, Arthur, why so angry?' he said.

'I'm giving you one chance,' Arthur said. 'Let Max go and undo this mess. Then you and the World Serpent can go away, somewhere where there are no people. And never come back.'

Loki laughed. 'One chance, eh? And what if I say no?'

'Then I'll defeat you.'

'Really? You and what army?'

'That one!' cried Arthur.

At that, the dead army attacked. Before Loki and the Jormungand knew what was happening, the Vikings were firing arrows at them. The iron-tipped weapons soared through the air. They seemed to hang there for a moment before falling. But each one of them bounced off the serpent's tough scales. Max put up his arms to protect himself from the arrows but slipped backwards in doing so. As he fell, he grabbed onto Loki's leg but only ended up pulling him down with him.

The two of them plunged towards the flood. More rain fell. And more arrows flew towards the Jormungand. One of the arrows was knocked off its course by one of the heavier drops. It sliced across Max's right thigh. He opened his mouth to scream, but he hit the water before any sound could emerge. Loki followed him into the flood.

Arthur saw what had happened to Max from his place on the plinth. He waved frantically at Bjorn, pointed at the small figure who had momentarily surfaced but then sunk again and yelled, 'He can't swim. Help him!'

Bjorn nodded and grunted orders to the soldiers. Half of them continued to fire arrows towards the serpent, while the other half rowed the boat around the Spire to where Max had fallen into the water. Bjorn threw his helmet to the deck then dived into the water. Arthur watched with bated breath.

Meanwhile, an arrow had managed to pierce one of the Jormungand's wings. The creature shrieked in pain and plunged downwards, but just before it hit the water it started to flap its damaged wing again, breaking its fall and landing gently on the surface of the flood. Seeing his opportunity, one sword-wielding Viking raced across the boat straight towards the Jormungand. He leaped off the side of the vessel and onto the beast's back, leaning over and plunging his blade deep into the serpent's tender underbelly. With another ear-piercing cry, the Jormungand flicked the Viking off with its tail, then crept back up the surface of the Spire, climbing this time rather than flying. The other Vikings continued to fire arrows at the retreating beast.

Bjorn found Max under the water, struggling to kick with his injured leg. A steady flow of bright red blood flowed out of the wound. The Viking clamped his hand over the cut to try and stop the bleeding then hooked his other arm round Max's chest. He kicked his legs and swam back to the surface. A couple of soldiers in the boat spotted Bjorn and the boy and reached over the edge to help them in. Max looked around him, taking in his surroundings as quickly as he could, then wrapped his arms around Bjorn in a tight hug.

From the plinth, Arthur breathed a sigh of relief,

but he barely had time to celebrate as he heard a terrible crashing sound behind him. He turned around to find Loki standing there, back in his true form. He'd ripped the statue off the plinth and raised it high above his head.

'Hi there!' he said cheerfully as he made to drop the statue on Arthur. Arthur was quick, however, and leapt backwards off the plinth. The statue smashed into pieces on impact just as Arthur grabbed hold of one of the ridges carved into the stone of the plinth. The hammer clattered out of his grip and into the water. He couldn't see where it had gone with the force of the raindrops causing the surface to leap and ripple.

The Vikings, meanwhile, continued firing arrows at the Jormungand, but only a few of them were sinking into its flesh. It screeched with each new wound, but the damage did not seem to be causing it any major problems. Bjorn put his helmet on Max's head; it was far too big for him but at least it would save him from any really critical injuries.

'Max! Max! Over here!' Max heard Ash's voice

calling him. He turned around and spotted her standing in the open window of the bookshop, waving at him.

'Ash!' he called back.

'Get under cover, Max!'

He nodded and looked around him. He found an abandoned metal shield, round, with the image of the Jormungand painted on it. He curled up on the deck and pulled the shield over himself, just in time.

Shrieking as it went, the Jormungand pushed off the top of the Spire and swooped downwards. It soared over the Viking boat, its wide mouth open, swallowing a handful of the soldiers whole as it went. Max could feel the force of the wind as it passed overhead. Some of the other soldiers swiped at it with their swords as it flew over, while the rest fired more arrows into its side. It retreated back upwards, soaring higher into the sky, hovering just above the Spire and out of reach of the arrows.

Meanwhile, Arthur was still clinging to the plinth when he heard Loki take a step towards him.

'Well, well, well,' he said. 'The great warrior falls so

early? That's unfortunate.' He thinks I'm in the water, Arthur realised. Loki stood right above him now, not even noticing him.

'Tricked you!' cried Arthur. He reached up and grabbed Loki's leg with one hand, pulling it out from under him. Loki landed heavily on his back and was momentarily stunned.

Arthur used the time to pull himself back up onto the plinth and as he knelt on it, panting to regain his breath, he noticed that the Jormungand, which had been hovering steadily in the sky, was plummeting downwards. But as Loki pulled himself back to his feet, the serpent suddenly pulled up from its unexpected dive and regained its original position over the Spire. Arthur looked down at Loki, wondering if the events were connected.

'You lied to us from day one,' Arthur said to him. 'You almost got us killed by drowning, cave-ins, explosions and being eaten by a giant snake. You put my father in the hospital. And you want to destroy the world. This ends here.'

'Oh, come on, Arthur!' said Loki, smiling. 'Before

you met me, you were weak. You were afraid of any adventure, you were shy, you wouldn't even speak up in class. But now, now you're leading an army! Granted, it's an army that can't possibly win, but you should still be thanking me.'

Before Arthur could react, Loki grabbed the collar of his tunic with one hand and lifted him off his feet. Arthur clawed at the fist but Loki was too strong and his vice-like grip wouldn't loosen. As he struggled, Arthur felt the pendant slapping against his chest.

'Just give up, Arthur – you can't beat me.'

'Oh yes, I can,' he said, grabbing the pendant, snapping its cord and flinging it at Loki. The Trickster God dropped Arthur when he realised what he was doing but it was too late – the pendant hit him full in the face. He was blasted backwards in a flash of green and onto the roof of a nearby newspaper vendor's metal hutch. In the sky, the Jormungand was also thrown backwards by an invisible force and screeched in rage.

It suddenly hit Arthur – Loki and the Jormungand were somehow linked. He wasn't sure how or why, but he was sure he could use that knowledge to help defeat them both. As Loki was squirming on the hut roof in pain, clutching his face, the World Serpent was writhing in the sky. Arthur picked up the pendant where it had bounced off Loki and tied it back around his neck. He looked down into the water and up at the dark-green rain clouds. He stepped back to the far edge of the plinth and then, with a deep breath, ran forward and jumped. As he soared over the floodwater, he closed his eyes, certain for a split second that he wasn't going to make it. But his feet landed right on the edge of the roof of the newspaper vendor's hutch.

'That *really* hurt!' complained Loki, looking up from where he lay. Arthur stood over him, just as Loki had stood over Arthur a few minutes ago.

'You should leave now,' Arthur said. 'Just go. Run away.'

Loki smiled as the green light flashed out of his eyes and stood up, towering over Arthur.

'That's a nice offer,' he said, 'but I'll have to refuse.' He picked Arthur up by the neck of his tunic and threw him over his head the way some people would throw away a ball of paper.

Arthur didn't so much as splash into the water as crash. The tarmac scratched Arthur's cheek when he bounced off the road underneath, cutting it open. He wanted to yell in pain but was worried about losing oxygen. Using what was left of his strength, he struggled back to the surface. The rain seemed to have gotten heavier now. The Vikings weren't really getting anywhere with the Jormungand: their arrows either fell short or bounced off its scales, and those that did pierce their target were still having little effect. Loki had returned to the plinth, which was higher than the roof of the hutch and still largely water free.

For a moment Arthur felt total despair – they were losing and losing badly. Then he heard Loki call out to the Jormungand, and when he looked at the creature Arthur saw that it was still hovering right above the Spire – the Spire with its sharp tip piercing the sky like a spear. It was bigger and stronger than anything the original Viking army would have had, and might be able to penetrate those tough scales. An idea flashed into his head – if he could only knock Loki down now, while he wasn't looking, and through that link make the serpent fall, then there was a chance that at least one of their opponents could be dealt with permanently. He looked around in desperation, but he had nothing to hit the god with.

Suddenly, Arthur felt something in his hand under the water. He lifted it out. The hammer was there, right in his grasp at the time when he needed it most. It felt lighter somehow and he rubbed the handle. He briefly wondered if something had guided the weapon to him, but then quickly turned his thoughts to the task at hand.

Arthur looked directly at Loki on the plinth. He had to hit him just right to make him fall straight down. He concentrated, then reached the hammer back behind his head and launched it with all the force he could manage. It tumbled through the air, turning as it went, and hit Loki square in the back, between the shoulder blades. With an anguished groan the god fell face forward into the flood.

As Loki fell, so did the Jormungand. It crashed

straight onto the Spire, which pierced its scales and went right through its cold heart. The Vikings stopped firing their arrows, Max came out from behind his shield, the people in the buildings stared through the windows and Arthur watched in awe as the creature screamed and writhed in agony, its wings flapping helplessly and its feet scrabbling at the air. After a moment the struggling subsided and finally the serpent was still, as Loki, floundering in the water, watched helplessly.

'No!' screeched Loki as the serpent died. Hot, salty tears ran down his scarred face. 'Nooooo!' His voice echoed off the buildings around them.

The body of the World Serpent shuddered before evaporating into a bright-green light. The light blazed so brilliantly that everyone had to look away. When they opened their eyes and looked back, all trace of the Jormungand was gone.

The rain had stopped also, which Arthur, still bobbing about in the water, was relieved to find. Or, rather, it had stopped momentarily because suddenly the drops started to flow upwards. Drop after drop, puddle after puddle, flood after flood: all the water in the street flowed up into the sky, retreating back into the green clouds. It flowed around Arthur as it went and he felt himself slowly sinking to the ground. It was like a bath emptying, only the bath in this case was the city of Dublin.

There was so much water under the Viking boat that it managed to pull the boat upwards with it. Bjorn, Max and the other Viking soldiers jumped out and into the lowering water. They watched as the waters pulled their boat towards the clouds.

As all the water retreated and the last drops flew back into the green clouds, the boat had nothing to suspend it any more. It fell back down to earth. The dead army ran out of its way, Bjorn carrying Max on his shoulders. The boat crashed onto the tarmac like the helicopter had earlier, exploding in a mess of wood splinters and metal.

The sky above was clear again and the sun was shining on the street as people started pouring out of the buildings. Arthur joined the army and Ash ran to them. Without a word, she hugged Max tightly, then turned to Arthur and flung her arms around him.

'You did it!' she said. 'You saved us all!' She kissed him on the cheek. When she pulled back from him, they both blushed and wouldn't meet each other's eyes.

'Not just me,' he managed eventually, 'them too.' He pointed to the surviving Vikings who were looking forlornly at their ruined boat.

'Hey,' interrupted Max, 'where's Loki?'

They looked around, searching the faces of the growing crowd: no sign of Loki in any of his guises anywhere. The only remaining trace of him was the hammer that had mysteriously reappeared at Arthur's feet.

'I don't know,' Arthur replied as he picked up the hammer, 'but all that matters now is that we won.' The three of them hugged each other as the spectators started to applaud.

Among the spectators was a young mother pushing a baby in a buggy. The baby – Little Aaron – had been crying all through the ordeal and only now, after the applause, did he stop wailing. She pinched his cheek adoringly.

'You're very quiet all of a sudden,' she said as she pushed the buggy away from the crowd, finally able to go home.

What she didn't know was that the real Little Aaron had been hidden behind a parked car and was crying his eyes out. The baby in the buggy heard the wailing and grinned.

CHAPTER TWENTY-TWO

It didn't take Arthur or Ash long to work out what to do with the dead army. Now that their boat and home for the past thousand years had been destroyed, it should have been a problem. But as it happened, Arthur, Ash and the boy they'd known as Will had visited the perfect place about a week beforehand.

Due to the destruction and inevitable confusion following the Jormungand's attack, the city of Dublin was more or less closed for business: no shops, museums or schools opened. So the dead army really had no problem climbing over the fake stone wall into the Viking Experience. Arthur, Ash and Max led them around the empty recreation village, showing them the little huts they could live in.

'As long as you don't move, just like those mannequins, when there are people about, you should be fine,' Arthur explained. 'No one will suspect that you're real Vikings at all. Just don't have any wild parties!'

Bjorn nodded and grunted his thanks.

'We'll come and visit you,' promised Arthur.

The entire army stood to attention and saluted the three children. They turned to leave but Arthur had one thing still on his mind.

'Bjorn?' he asked. 'I had a dream. And they said in it that when Loki was to escape it would mean Ragnarok. Do you know what that is – Ragnarok?'

Fear had crept into Bjorn's eyes at the mention of the word. He sadly nodded.

'What is it, Bjorn?'

Bjorn opened his mouth and tried to form the words, but only grunts came out. He stood there looking frustrated until Ash had a brainwave. 'Pen and paper, we need a pen and paper. He can write it down.'

Frantically they patted down their pockets but

all they came up with was a soggy piece of tissue in Ash's pocket – no pen or pencil. Then one of the other Viking soldiers appeared with a piece of burnt stick. Bjorn took the stick and used the blackened end to draw some runes on the ground. Arthur looked at the runes and clutched the pendant in his hand. The other two children looked at him expectantly. 'It says the end of the world,' he said, then added with a rueful smile, 'again.'

Arthur, Ash and Max arrived home a couple of hours later, having retrieved their bikes from outside the Metro site. The Barry family were sitting around the living-room TV when they came in, still in their pyjamas, glued to the news.

'Have you seen this?' exclaimed Mr Barry. 'They're saying on the news that some giant snake thing attacked the city.'

'Hold on,' said Stace, suspiciously eyeing-up Arthur's tunic, 'where have you lot been?'

'Yes, actually!' said Mrs Barry, tearing herself away from the TV. 'Where have you been? And what's wrong with your leg, Max? Is that blood? And Arthur, what happened to your face?'

The three children looked at each other, then at the adults, then told the story they'd rehearsed in unison.

'We went for an early game of football and a dog took our ball and we chased it, but Arthur tripped and fell and scratched his face and the dog bit Max's leg.'

'What?' shrieked Mrs Barry. 'Whose dog? I've a good mind to call the police –'

'Calm down, Mom,' said Ash, as Max said, 'I'm fine, really. It's not that bad.'

'We didn't recognise the dog, Mrs Barry,' said Arthur. 'I think it may have been a stray, and it ran off after we got the ball back.'

'Well, if you're certain. But that bite looks like it might need stitches, Max. And probably a tetanus shot as well.' Max groaned at the thought of an injection. Mrs Barry pointed to Arthur and Ash. 'You two go and get cleaned up and I'll take Max to the hospital. Arthur, be sure and clean that cut properly.'

'Wait!' Stace stopped her. 'Aren't you curious as to why Arthur is wearing that crazy get-up?'

'No,' Mrs Barry said, ushering Max back out the door, 'and it's rude to call someone's clothes a "crazy get-up", young lady.'

Arthur and Ash rushed upstairs before Stace could ask any more awkward questions. Exhausted, they quickly fell asleep on the floor of Ash's bedroom, huddled together on some spare couch cushions.

※※※※

As they slept on, someone else, in a different part of the country, was watching the news. She took great interest in the story of the giant snake. The news report was showing the only video footage they had of the scene, taken from the third floor of the bookshop on O'Connell Street on a mobile phone. She hit a button on her remote. The image freeze-framed. She knelt down on the soft-carpeted floor and put her face right next to the screen. Although the image was distorted and pixelated from this close, it was clear that what she was seeing was right. A boy, possibly twelve or thirteen years old, dressed in authentic Viking clothes and throwing a war hammer at a grown man. She vowed to find out exactly who this boy was and everything she could about him.

Arthur and Ash would have slept right through the day if Mrs Barry hadn't knocked on the door, waking them.

'Arthur,' she said, 'that nice young garda was just on the phone. Your father woke up this morning.'

Arthur sat up straight. 'He did? Is he coming home?'

'Not yet, dear. The hospital wants to keep an eye on him for a few more days. But the garda said he'll pick you up in a while if you want to visit your dad.'

Arthur leaped out of bed, grabbed the hammer and raced across the street to his house. He busied himself by tidying up and taking a hot shower. An hour later Garda Morrissey was at his door. When the garda led Arthur into the hospital ward, Joe was sitting up in bed. His right leg was now in a stiff cast and the swelling in his face had subsided but he was still badly bruised. Arthur hugged him tightly without saying a word. Joe winced.

'Sorry,' said Arthur, stepping back.

'It's okay,' Joe said, holding his ribs. 'I'm just a bit delicate. Anyway, I'm glad I'm still around to feel the hug at all. So, what did I miss?'

'Oh, nothing,' Arthur replied, 'just a giant snake almost destroying Dublin.'

'Same old, same old.' Joe pointed to his face. 'You look like you've been in the wars yourself.'

'Oh, this, it's nothing, I just fell over my own feet while playing football.'

'So what do you reckon?' said Joe, this time pointing at his own face. 'Will I still need a mask next week?'

'What's next week?'

'Hallowe'en.'

'Oh yeah. I completely forgot.'

Across the city, the real Little Aaron was reunited with his mother. She could have sworn he was in the buggy as she pushed it away from the scene of all the action. Later on, she had joined a group of people watching the news of the serpent in a TV-shop window. The pictures on the screen were shocking, but not as shocking as it had been in real life. When she'd had enough and decided to head for home, she had found that the buggy was empty.

Luckily, some good Samaritan had found Aaron on O'Connell Street and, after some frantic phone calls to the gardaí, her son was back in her arms.

※※※※※

The story of the giant snake soon spread all over the world. The only video footage that existed of it had been taken on low-resolution mobile phones. Eyewitness accounts were featured on every news station in the world. Many of them mentioned the mysterious young boy who'd been spotted on O'Connell Street carrying a hammer.

Arthur, Ash and Max had decided not to fill their parents in on their part in the serpent incident. In fact, they didn't want to fill anyone in. They thought it was all over until Ash and Max went trick-or-treating to Arthur's on Hallowe'en.

Joe had been home for two days and life was getting back to normal. Ruairí and Deirdre had called over to see how he was doing. They were just leaving and he was leading them out to the door on his crutches.

'Thanks for coming, guys,' he said. 'Any plans for tonight?'

'Well …' started Deirdre, blushing.

'We're going on a date,' finished Ruairí.

'A date?' Joe seemed surprised. 'That's great! I'm glad to hear it.'

As they walked down the driveway, Max and Ash were walking up.

'Hello you two. What are you dressed as, Max?' Joe asked when he saw them.

'I'm a Viking!' exclaimed Max cheerfully. He'd made a tunic out of an old black sheet he'd found under their stairs and a pendant and helmet out of tin foil. He also carried a sword he'd constructed from tin foil and cardboard.

'That's great, Max!' said Joe. 'What about you, Ash? No costume?'

'No,' she said. 'I didn't really feel like dressing up this year.'

'Same as Arthur. He's in the living room watching TV. Come on in.'

As Joe filled up Max's goodie bag in the hallway with sweets and nuts, balancing precariously on his good leg, Ash asked Arthur how he was feeling.

'Not bad,' he said. 'I didn't have a nightmare last night, which was a bonus. And this hasn't been glowing.' He held up the pendant from around his neck. 'So that's probably a good sign too.'

'Have you worked out what that hammer is yet?'

It was stored under his bed. 'No idea. But it helped defeat Loki so it has to be a good thing.'

'Hey,' said Joe, swinging back into the room and looking at the TV, 'who's that guy?'

An American cartoon had been playing but now the screen was full of Loki's face. It was an extreme close-up of the younger Loki, unscarred and with a neatly trimmed beard and clean hair. As always, he was grinning.

Arthur, Ash and Max looked at each other.

'That's –' Ash began.

'My name is Loki,' Loki's voice said from the TV set. 'Right now, I'm speaking to everyone in the world. Everyone can see or hear this message. The entire world.' His grin disappeared now. 'Remember that giant snake that attacked Dublin? Well, now you don't. You will all forget about it: forget it ever happened, forget the eyewitness accounts and the descriptions of the serpent. Just forget. And I want you to forget me too. Forget my face, forget my voice, forget you ever saw me on here tonight. You see, it's very difficult to be an evildoer if people are expecting you.'

He leaned forward, nearer the camera that was on him, going out of focus as he did. 'I want you all to forget. All of you. Except three people: Arthur Quinn and Ash and Max Barry. I want you three to remember. Because I want to haunt your dreams. And I want you three to know that sometime, somehow, when you're least expecting it, I'm coming to get you.'

He sat back again and the camera refocused on him. 'Well, that's all from me for now. Goodnight, world.'

The transmission shut off and the cartoon flickered back into life. Arthur looked at Ash; Ash looked at Max.

'Dad?' Arthur asked. 'Did you hear about the giant snake?'

'What giant snake?' replied Joe.

'The giant serpent, Dad. That attacked Dublin.'

'Oh wait,' Joe said, smiling, 'is this some kind of Hallowe'en joke? No, I didn't hear about the giant snake.' He waited for the punchline, but instead Arthur turned to his friends.

'Well, it looks like Loki's little trick has worked,' he said. Ash and Max looked at him, worried. 'But,' he continued, brightening up, 'I'm not too concerned. I've got two great friends and an army at my disposal. What more could a twelve-year-old boy want?'

Joe looked confused. 'That's not much of a punchline.'

'No,' said Arthur, 'no, it's not. But it's true.'

And with that, Arthur, Ash and Max burst out laughing.

EPILOGUE

Loki left the TV studio, pulling the collar up on his grey blazer. He walked away, forgotten and unseen. They may have beaten him once but they wouldn't do it again. He already knew how to defeat them next time. It would be so easy to destroy the world. All he had to do was follow the howl of the wolf.